SLEEPING WITH THE ENEMY

SLEEPING WITH THE ENEMY

Clarissa Johnson

Published by A Light of Hope Enterprises
PO Box 487
Rincon, GA 31326
www.clarissajohnson.com
*Previously published by Pink Kiss Publishing Company

ISBN-13: 978-0-9889270-0-1
Library of Congress Control Number: 2013906638

Cover Design & Interior Layout by A'ndrea J. Wilson for Divine Garden Press www.divinegardenpress.com
Cover Photo © Sergei Razvodovskij | Dreamstime.com

This book is affectionately dedicated to my late grandmother, Mamie Gibson.

Grandma Mamie, you have always been my, and all of your children/grandchildren biggest supporter. I miss you dearly and I wish you were here to share in this joyous moment with me. However, I can visualize you sitting in heaven chewing your Taylor Pride, shaking your head and saying, "Umph, umph, umph—that Clarissa is somebody. Shonuff!" Oh… to hear you say those words made me feel like I could do anything. So to you, granny, I dedicate my first novel. Although you're gone, you will never be forgotten. I love you!

Acknowledgments

First I would like to give honor to God, who is truly the author of this book. He just used me as an instrument to write the story. Only He can take what we would consider a mess and create a message of hope, love and redemption.

To my husband, Dale, who has selflessly supported me through this journey. You never cease to amaze me. I am extremely proud of you and all that you have accomplished within the last year. I am so honored to be your wife. You are my rock and I love you more than you will ever know.

To my daughters, Claranesia and Kennae, I love you both so much. You have given me so much joy, and I am so proud to be your mom. I expect nothing but greatness from the both of you. As my grandmother use to say to me, I say to you— you are somebody!

To my mom, Gwendolyn, you are the best mother a girl could ask for. In you I have a friend, a confidant, a counselor, a cheer-leader, and prayer partner. I have learned so much from you and I would not be who I am today, without you and your unconditional love.

To my father, Clarence, thank you for your strict love. I didn't like it back then, but I so appreciate it now. I love you daddy!

To my step-mother, Sarah, I have never considered you as a mere stepmom. You have always treated me as your own. Thank you for all you've done for me and my girls. I love you just as much as I love my natural mom. You have been my example of what a stepmom should be.

With that being said, I would like to acknowledge my stepchildren. Thank you for welcoming me into your circle, and I hope that I can be half the stepmother to you as mine are to me. And Tyeshia, you will always be my boo!

To my siblings, Stanvoski, Derea, Troy, Tamika and Olesia, although different moms and dads, I love each one of you. I wish you nothing but the best.

To my cousin, Regina, thank you for being there whenever I needed to bounce an idea off of you. I appreciate all of your suggestions and input along the way.

To my sister-friend, Bridget, there are not enough words to say what you mean to me. You deserve a page all by yourself. You have taught, and are still teaching me what it truly means to be a friend. Thank you for always being there, and thank you for not giving up.

To my girlfriends, Pam, Kim, Ericka, Emerald and Camone, although I met you all in different seasons, I have learned so much from you ladies and you have impacted my life tremendously. Your ministry of friendship has truly been a blessing to me.

To my mother-in-law, Barbara, you are the best mother-in-law ever! Thank you for embracing me as one of your own.

To my sister-in-laws, Keia and Tawana, thank you for welcoming into your family and making me feel apart. Oh yeah, and thanks for all the laughs.

Raymond and Schelene, there are no words that can describe the love we have for you. You have been such a blessing to me and my family. Thanks for all the support, the love, the prayers, and the counsel and advice you give. Everything you do is truly appreciated.

To my New Harvest Outreach and Abiding In The Word church families, this is where it all began, and I am truly grateful for your love and support. Elder Clark and Sis. Trudy, your influence and teachings really made a difference in my life. You pushed me so far outside my comfort zone and I learned things about myself that I never knew. I also learned I had gifts and talents that I never knew I had. Thanks, mom and dad!

T. D. Jakes, I don't know if you will ever read this book, but I want to thank you for the countless words you speak into my spirit. I have learned and gained so much knowledge from you, and the one thing I want to thank you for is—teaching me to think outside the box, yet to live inside the scriptures.

To my classmates of the Ministry in Training program of New Mercies Christian Church, Candice, Theresa, Curtis, Ken, Phil, James, CJ, Lawrence and Jeanette, thank you for your love and support through my transition. You guys are the best and I can't wait to walk down the aisles of New Mercies together next year. I'm so proud of each one of you.

Betty, you are the bomb ministry administrator. You make things happen. Thank you for the time you spent helping me with this book project. Your talent and skills are exceptional.

Armetria and Crystal, I'm in awe of the love and support you have shown me. It's amazing how God put you in my life, and to think, we have never met in person. You guys have been such wonderful "distant friends" and I just want to thank you so much for the seed you sown into this book. Your generosity is beyond words, and I am truly grateful.

A'ndrea Wilson, my own angel, sent by God. From day one, you unselfishly offered your knowledge and expertise. I am truly honored to have you as a mentor and a friend. Thanks for your impeccable work on this project.

Princess, I dare not end this without telling you how blessed I am to have met you. Thank you for your willingness to help me, and thank you for being on my team.

To my entire family, and host of friends, it is virtually impossible for me to list everyone who has impacted my life along this journey. Regardless if your name are listed here or not, does not in any way diminish your value in my life. I love and thank God for you all.

Stay Hopeful,

Clarissa

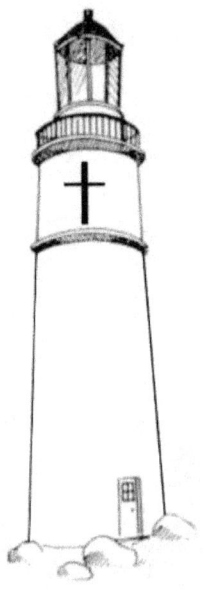

Lighthouses were created with a purpose.

Lighthouses symbolize safety, guidance & integrity.

Lighthouses provide hope & vision.

Lighthouses exist because storms & darkness exists.

Lighthouses are a perfect example of…

Clarissa Johnson
"A source of light in times of darkness"

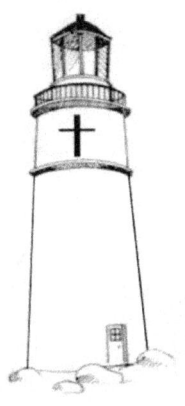

Prologue

Warrenton High School, Class of 1992 was preparing for their ten-year class reunion, and was getting ready to call their second planning meeting to order. Surprisingly, the majority of the class was in attendance, with the exception of the few that lived too far out of town to travel the few hours distance. Regardless of the few absences, this meeting was far more successful than the first one, a month ago, when only five people out of a class of seventy-one showed up.

This was a big deal to Cherise because—out of all the graduating classes of WHS, hers, the Class of 1992, was the most trifling. Unlike all the other classes, they didn't leave a positive last impression on the school. If rewards were given out, they would have been the class voted, "most likely not to succeed."

It wasn't that the class wasn't capable—they were actually a smart bunch. They attended school every day and did their assignments for the most part. However, they never worked to their full potentials because school was not their primary focus—having fun was. They spent most of their time partying, drinking, and playing spades. Oh, they lived for a good game of spades.

The most disappointing thing to Cherise about her graduating class was that they didn't go on a senior class trip, and for a moment there, it didn't appear that they were going to have a class reunion either, due to the lack of participation—as always. When Cherise got the call about the second meeting, she was thrilled. Looks like things were finally coming together for the Class of 92, and there was no way she was going to miss this meeting.

Everyone was truly enjoying themselves, having a great time socializing and reminiscing, with the exception of Terrell. He wasn't a graduate of the class, and his only purpose for being at the meeting, was to keep a secure watch on Cherise's every move. She was extremely annoyed by Terrell's presence, but refused to let him keep her from enjoying herself. She decided to leave him sitting in a corner alone, and walked around the room greeting old classmates she hadn't seen since graduation.

Terrell Tillman was what most women would describe as tall, dark and handsome; and he knew it. He had milk chocolate skin that was accented with hazel brown eyes, and a nice build. He always kept his naturally curly hair cut low, and with the exception of the weekends he had monthly drills with the Army National Guard, he kept his facial hair groomed very neatly. He was definitely known to turn quite a few heads whenever he walked into a room.

With today being clear, sunny and bright, he accessorized his white linen outfit with a flashy pair of Ray Ban shades. They only made him look even sexier than he already was. Cherise laughed to herself when she noticed how the women stared at her husband, and thought about how she used to look at him in that same way—but that was a long time ago. He no longer appealed to her as tall, dark and handsome. These past eight years had allowed her to see him in a totally different light. So while others were fascinated with Terrell's outer appearance, she had come to know a different side of him, and that prevailed over his good looks any day. *"Never judge a book by its cover"*, she recalled her grandmother saying.

Everybody loved Cherise because of her exuberant personality. Although a little on the thick side, she was quite a sexy woman. She only stood 5 feet 2 inches, but there was something about the way she carried herself with complete and total confidence. She had pretty long hair, but often wore it up in different French rolls and bun styles. She was a pretty girl, but not too pretty that she couldn't get her hands dirty and enjoy life. She knew how to be classy, but if push came to shove, she could also change a tire—something she learned from her father. He didn't want her ever stranded, without knowing what to do, in the case she ever had a flat.

Just as she figured, Terrell was watching every move she made. This aggravated her, and it was also the very reason she told him not to come in the first place. Who could enjoy themselves with someone stalking their every move? He watched everywhere she walked, everyone she hugged, and everyone she conversed with. He even monitored how close she let her body come in contact to the other person's body; especially if it was a dude. He literally timed how long she communicated with the men versus the women, and even made mental notes of Cherise's body language during each conversation she held.

He had already told her that he didn't like her hugging men after church, so what made her think it was okay to hug any of these guys? As far as he was concerned, all men were sneaky, and he didn't trust any of them; nor Cherise for that matter. She had probably dated a few of them back in the day, and if they got too close, old feelings might rekindle. *This is probably the reason she didn't want me to come anyway. Just so she could get her groove on with one of her ex-boyfriends. She thinks I'm stupid, but she won't be leaving with any of them today.* To Terrell, his thoughts were normal, and they were right on point.

After watching Terrell's facial expressions and his fidgetiness from across the room, Cherise's emotions immediately went into defense mode. *Uuuuuggggghhhhh! He gets on my mother-freaking nerves!* Becoming more irritated with each passing moment, she continued to argue with herself. *I ought to just leave him over there by his freaking self, because I told him not to come.* Responding to her own thoughts, she internally declared, *I didn't come here to sit in a freaking corner.* She stood still and battled with her feet to not go in Terrell's direction. Just the thought of sitting in a corner on a leash made her even angrier.

Cherise rolled her eyes at the sight of her stalking husband and turned her back. *Got-darn-it! This is some real bull-crap.* This was her way of cussing without using profanity. For some reason, she felt as long as she didn't say the actual cuss words, she was okay. However, God had been dealing with her on this issue. *God, why did you allow him to come here?* Cherise already knew God was not going to answer her, but she had developed her own special relationship with Him, so she knew she could let Him in on what she was feeling and thinking.

As she continued silently arguing with herself and talking to God, she humbled herself and finally decided to head back to where Terrell sat—just to pacify him. She figured she had been gone long enough to make him wish he never came, and maybe, just maybe, he would get bored, and decide to leave. She honestly didn't care about how he felt—she just didn't feel like arguing with him later on.

She was on her way to where he was sitting when she heard someone scream, "FIRE", and noticed smoke was filling the room quite rapidly. One by one, everybody began to pass out, except her. Trying to not panic, Cherise pulled her cell phone out of her purse and dialed 911. After giving the emergency representative the location and all other pertinent information requested, she decided to try and drag as many victims as she could outside, away from the building. She figured she might not be able to save everyone, but she would at least die trying.

Naturally, she started with the first person she came in contact with, but as she reached out to touch him, she got shocked. She tried again, but the exact same thing happened. She didn't quite know what was causing such a static reaction, but there was no time to waste. Cherise moved to another classmate and tried again, but the cycle continued to repeat itself. It was like she was in a real life virtual video game, and had to pass this stage in order to get to the next level. Her time was running out, and she hadn't been able to successfully pull anyone out of the burning building.

After a few unsuccessful attempts, she finally decided to run across the room and see if she could get any response, and maybe some assistance from Terrell, but he was completely unresponsive. Without missing a beat, she bent over and grabbed him under both arms, and to her surprise, she was able to haul him to safety. Without delay, she went right back inside, and pulled another person to safety. She continued this cycle until all victims were saved.

Cherise was exhausted and needed something to quench her thirst. Her heartbeat was racing like the cars in the Indy 500. She sat straight up in the bed and realized she had just had a dream—but it seemed so real. Out of all the dreams she had ever had, this one was completely different. She knew that this was more than just a dream. She knew that this one had some kind of a spiritual meaning, and it bothered her that she couldn't quite figure it out. She arose from the bed, put on her robe and went into the den to search her library of books for her dream and symbols book. She wanted to look up the word *fire*; to see if that would help her put together the pieces of her dream.

It was now three o'clock in the morning, and she had spent approximately two hours searching and seeking for answers. She finally decided to go back to bed, but still couldn't sleep. There were too many questions in her head that needed answers. Thinking about the dream—she knew that she was put in a position to be a lifesaver, but what she couldn't understand was why she kept getting shocked? Why did she have to pull Terrell out of the building first, before she could save everyone else? What did the fire represent? Hell, perhaps? Were they all in hell?

All she could think about was this dream, and made a mental note to call her pastor just as soon as she thought he was awake. Everything within her told her that this dream had a deeper meaning. This was one dream, she just couldn't ignore.

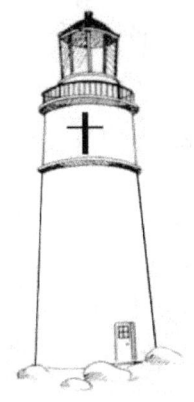

Chapter One

ONE YEAR LATER

Pastor Charles Revenew had just finished altar call and was preparing to give the benediction when Ronald Dukes stood up and stepped into the aisle with his right hand raised. He motioned like a child in class would do when asking for permission to speak. Ronald was a recovering addict and other than the few times he'd visited New Harvest Christian Center, hadn't attended church since he was a young boy, and didn't know anything about protocol, or church etiquette.

Ronald was in his mid-fifties, and the constant use of alcohol and drugs had really taken a toll on his physical appearance. His face was wrinkled, which made him look much older than he actually was. Large red puss bumps decorated his forehead and cheeks like polka dots, and his eyes were always red and dreary. One could question if he indeed, was on the road to recovery.

As he approached the front of the church, the pastor walked down the stairs of the pulpit to meet him at the altar. Unsure of what the shabby man wanted, Pastor Revenew leaned down and discreetly asked him his business. There was protracted silence throughout the entire sanctuary as everyone watched the scene before them. Ronald whispered back in the pastor's ear, and in response, the pastor passed him the microphone and gestured to him to speak.

Ronald thanked the pastor and spoke boldly into the mic. "I've been coming to this church for a few weeks now and I have really been enjoying myself. I have been learning a lot of things that I didn't know about God and about His love. All my life I've searched for a love like this. I searched for it in women, alcohol, drugs and although I'm ashamed to say it, I've even searched for it in other men. No matter where I looked for it, I just couldn't seem to ever find it. I never really knew that someone could love *(pointing to himself)* me, the way you say God loves me."

Now although Ronald's outer appearance was jacked up, his dialect was surprisingly impressive. Even in his poor-like state, his baritone voice demanded attention, and for the most part, he spoke with intelligence and in complete sentences. Without being intimidated by the crowd, he continued...

"At one time, I had it going on. I had a nice home, nice cars, a great job, and I even graduated with a BA in Business Management. While on my search for love, I found myself involved with the wrong crowds. In the beginning, everything was cool, but after a period of time, things got way out of hand. I was partying, drinking, and trying all types of drugs. I thought I could handle it, but I guess it was handling me. Somewhere I got caught up and I lost everything.

"A few weeks ago, I was sitting in my room with thoughts of suicide running through my mind. I'm not sure how I got to this place, but I had reached my lowest and I had no desire to continue to live. After several hours of crying, I decided to take a walk to see if I could clear my mind. I had no intention of coming to church, but as I walked past the building, I could hear a woman singing, and although I couldn't make out what she was singing about, the voice drew me closer and closer to the door.

"I stood outside for several minutes before entering, and I could hear this woman talking about being heavily weighted down by situations, past hurts and mistakes; and sometimes feeling like wanting to give up. I can't explain it, but it was as if she was talking directly to me. After a few more minutes, I came in and sat in the back of the church. Then, as I was sitting there, she began to sing the words—*like the dew in the morning, gently rest upon my heart.* The more she sang, the better I began to feel. I can't quite explain what I was feeling, but I know it felt better than any drug or alcohol I've ever experienced."

Looking through the small crowd at the nodding of heads and waving of hands, he could tell that many others could relate to what he was speaking about. He continued to gaze the audience until he spotted Cherise, then he continued…

"Sis. Cherise, I want to let you know that I think you have an amazing voice and gift. You have no idea what you did for me, but you saved my life that night. It was that night, that I decided to give my life to Christ and for that, I would like to say thank you from the bottom of my heart."

Turning to look at the pastor, he teased, "I've been around a long time, and I have seen a lot of things, so I don't fool with preachers too funny, but I think you're a good man. I really enjoy listening to you preach, and if it's alright with you Pastor, I would like to become a member of your church."

The congregation roared in praises as the pastor hugged Ronald and gave him the right hand of fellowship. Others stood in line, waiting their turn to hug and welcome Ronald to the church family, as the musicians played the church's welcoming anthem. Cherise had created a song, entitled, "We Welcome You to New Harvest", inspired by the tune of "Lord of the Harvest", by gospel singing artist, Fred Hammond. They normally sung it for new visitors, but the musicians liked the tune so much, they played it when new members joined the church as well.

After the pastor gave the benediction, he walked throughout the small church greeting everyone as he always does every Sunday after service. As Cherise was getting ready to hug the pastor, Terrell stepped up behind her, and in an angry tone said, "I'm ready to go." Cherise was amazed at his rudeness, and rolled her eyes in disgust. She hugged the pastor and told him how much she enjoyed the today's message, and turned to locate her children.

Cherise had two beautiful daughters. Alyson, whom for no other reason than the spelling of the name, Cherise named after the 80s R&B Singer, Alyson Williams, known for her songs, "I Need Your Lovin'" and "Just Call My Name", was eleven and getting ready to start Middle School. Little Alysa had just turned three. She wasn't named after anyone in particular, but Cherise just thought it would be too cute to have both of her daughters' names be similar.

Terrell loved both of their daughters, but whenever he was mad with Cherise, he took it out on Alyson. This was only because Alyson was not his own flesh and blood, and he knew that mistreating her would hurt Cherise more than anything else. He knew that her children were her treasure, and with them was where her heart lies.

Alyson acknowledged Terrell as her daddy and loved him just as much or even more than Stan, her real father. She knew Stan, but didn't have a father-daughter relationship with him, as she did with Terrell. Terrell helped her with homework, gave her an allowance, and let her play-play drive when riding down the highway. It wasn't that often but, he would even punish her whenever she was disobedient.

After gathering up the kids, Cherise hurried toward the car where Terrell sat waiting. She could tell by the look on his face that this was not going to be a pleasant ride. The drive home usually took about forty-five minutes, and she dreaded the lecture awaiting her in the car. As soon as they pulled out of the church's parking lot, Terrell looked at her with a look of disgust and questioned, "You must be messing around with that guy Ronald or something?"

Shocked, Cherise responded with a high pitched tone, "WHAT? Are you serious? Are you seriously sitting up here accusing me of messing around with that man?"

"You got to be! Because why would he call your name out of the *whole* praise team? You're not the only one that sings," Terrell shouted. "Better yet, how does he even know your name? Tell me that, Cherise."

In her mind, Cherise sarcastically responded; *he knows my name because he calls it every time we sleep together, you dummy.* However, she didn't want to speak that lie out loud, but she figured a stupid question deserved a stupid answer. He knew darn well that not only was her name called out during service every Sunday for one thing or another, but it was also on the church's program under the Ministries in the church.

Cherise knew she shouldn't entertain Terrell, but he was getting on her last nerve. This was worse than the time he accused her of messing with Marcus, a little fourteen-year old boy that she taught in Sunday school. "I'm so sick of you accusing me of freaking EVERYBODY and ANYBODY. I'm no Halle Berry, but I don't have to settle for just anybody! If you're gonna give me somebody, then give me somebody! Give me a Morris Chestnut kind of guy. Heck, I'll even take a Flava Flav kind of guy, but don't be pushing me off on some OLD, DRUNKEN, ADDICT!" Cherise yelled.

She immediately felt bad for her choice of words and the manner in which she spoke about Ronald. He was a newly converted Christian and didn't deserve to be labeled as such. Cherise was glad no one else was around to witness her outburst, especially Ronald.

"What makes you think that your singing is more powerful than anyone else?" Terrell asked. He then changed his voice in a way to imitate and mock Ronald. "Sis. Cruse really has an amazing voice. Sis. Cruse has an awesome gift. Sis. Cruse saved my life." Switching back to his own voice, "Yeah right. You think I don't know game when I hear it?" Terrell questioned, but said more like a statement, while gazing over at Cherise.

"How dare you take that man's testimony and turn it into some type of sick lie. I will not apologize for the gift God placed inside of me, nor will I apologize for Him using me for His Glory."

As Terrell continued to talk to him-self, because at this time, Cherise had tuned him out and turned her face to look out the passenger window. As she gazed at the trees passing by, she stroked her fingers across the cross on her necklace. No matter what she wore, the necklace was always a part of her attire. It didn't make any bold fashion statement, but it spoke volumes of comfort to her whenever she needed it.

Her grandmother had given her the necklace many years ago, after she had left Alyson's father. He had constantly threatened her, which left her afraid for her life. Ms. Mamie, short in stature but full of the Holy Ghost, had rubbed the cross down with olive oil that had been prayed over by the Pastor and Elders of the church, and prayed a prayer of protection over the life of Cherise and her kids. Although her grandmother had passed away, the words she spoke still lived within her heart. *"Baby, this necklace represents my love for you, and God's love for us. Anything you need is at the cross.*

"Any worries, any fears you face, any concerns or cares you have, you can cast them upon the Lord. For the Bible declares, He cares for you, and he knoooooooows, just what you're going through, baby. I might not always be here, but He is always with you."

After she finished speaking, she started singing softly, words of comfort. *"Tis so sweet, to trust in Jesus. Just to take Him at His word. Just to rest upon His promise. Just to know, thus says the Lord."*

It didn't take much for Ms. Mamie to get excited whenever she was talking about Her Lord. Feeling the spirit, she took it an octave higher. *"Jeeeeesuuus Jesus. How I trust Him. How I proved Him, o'er and o'er. Jesus Jesus, precious Jesus. O for graaaaace, to trust Him more."* Wiping tears of joy that had fallen down her cheeks, Ms. Mamie continued... *"Yes suh! He is faithful, baby. He can do anything! All you gotta do is trust Him."*

Tears filled Cherise's eyes as she remembered her grandmother and her words. Still looking out the window, she silently prayed, *"Lord, I need you! Please help me!"*

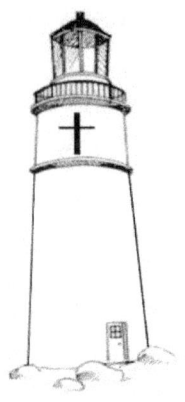

Chapter Two

Cherise couldn't wait to get home and get out of the car with Terrell. She had heard just about enough of his senseless remarks and would soon explode if she didn't get a way of escape pronto. This was one of the main reasons she hardly rode with him to church in the first place.

They could never ride home together without arguing about something—nothing really. Of course, if they could ride together, they would have less wear and tear on both vehicles, and not to mention the amount of money on fuel they would save. Any other time, those things didn't even matter to Cherise but this week, her funds were low, and she needed to save her tank of gas to travel back and forth to work until Thursday—payday.

Cherise was so aggravated and deep in thought that she forgot all about getting Alysa out of the booster seat. As soon as the car pulled into the driveway, not even fully parked, she opened her door, jumped out, slammed the door, and went in the house, straight to her bedroom. Alyson, however, was on her game. She was such a big helper. She unbuckled Alysa and made sure her little sister entered the house safely. Alyson was young, but she knew when something was bothering her mom, and knew how to give her the space she needed to recoup.

After entering the house, Alyson went to the kitchen, washed her hands, and fixed her and her baby sister a sandwich and some juice. Alysa had already gone into the bedroom and turned on the TV, which was already set on their favorite channel, *The Disney Channel.* Today, they were playing a marathon of *That's So Raven,* and even though there was a significant age difference between the two girls, they both enjoyed the program with the same excitement. This would definitely keep them engaged for at least a couple of hours.

Cherise was now in the bathroom preparing to take a hot bubble bath. This was therapeutic for her, and it also gave her the alone time she needed to think, cry, and talk to God. While the water was running, she plugged up her portable CD player and put on some smooth jazz. To ensure no disturbances from the kids, and especially Terrell, she locked the door, took off her clothes, and slid her tense body down in the hot steamy tub.

After relaxing her head on her bath pillow, her thoughts took off on a roller coaster ride. They didn't play in any particular order; they were actually all over the place. The thrilling ride started off kind of slow, climbing a steep hill as she thought about when she and Terrell first met.

It was like a dream come true. She had recently escaped an abusive relationship with Alyson's father, so the special attention she received from Terrell was like a drug. She was addicted. She couldn't get enough of it. He was kind and considerate, soft and gentle, and attentive. He was a great kisser, and he was oh-so-good in bed.

After six months of dating and living together, Terrell was forced to tell Cherise his best kept secret. He would have kept it longer, but he wasn't the one who was pulling all the strings. When his wife found out about his new beau, she began to make his life a living hell. Not because she wanted him back, but because he hadn't paid her any child support for their daughter in several months. The way she figured it, she would be damned if he spent all his money on a new woman and her child, and not take care of his own.

Had he told Cherise he was still married, he knew she wouldn't have given him the time of day, which was the exact reason he didn't tell her. The only thing that justified their relationship was the fact that Terrell and his wife had been separated for over two years before they even met.

As much as the news of Terrell's wife bothered her, Cherise was in too deep. She had already developed strong feelings for him, and walking away was easier said than done, so she decided to stay with him. She often wondered if she was she being punished for taking up with a married man. I mean, it wasn't like they were really together anymore. His wife had moved on and was living with another man herself. She made it quite clear that, if and when the time came for a divorce, Terrell would be the one to file, and to pay.

Although Cherise was not saved yet, she always had morals, and living in that type of situation indefinitely, was definitely not an option. It was only a few months later that she attended her uncle's church for a revival, and accepted Christ as her personal savior. Immediately after church, she went home and told Terrell her good news. She also told him that she would not continue living in sin with him. She gave him the ultimatum of finalizing his divorce and marrying her, or moving out and on with his life. No matter his objections, she stood firm on her decision.

Right after they were married, Terrell decided he would also get saved. The only thing is, when Terrell accepted Christ, there was a change—not for the better—for the worse.

Cherise couldn't understand it because—they both went to the same church, attended the same Bible study classes, and were taught by the same pastor. However, you would have sworn that Terrell was a member of a different church, better yet, a different religion.

He was real cocky, puffed up, and had become very disrespectful towards leadership. He had gained his own revelation of what a Christian was, and how a Christian should live. Nobody, and I mean nobody, could tell him anything.

One night when they were having an in-home Bible study at their house, Terrell got mad because no one would agree with his interpretation of a particular scripture. He told everyone, "This is my house, and what I say goes. If you don't like it, you can get to stepping." They did just that.

For a brief moment, Cherise thought about the comedy TV show, *Martin*. She giggled at the memory of how the actor, Martin Lawrence, would use the same words when throwing his friends out of his house. Entertaining herself, she did her best Martin impersonation, "Get to stepping!" That just tickled her; however, that funny intermission didn't last long. Another incident came to mind...

Pastor Revenew had requested to meet with them after services one Sunday. He normally would have met with them individually, but since this concerned both of them, he requested both of their presence in the meeting. He began by telling Terrell he had noticed within the past few months, that he had made some major upgrades on his new truck. Terrell was a big flaunter, and he loved to show off, so everybody knew about his new big tires and shiny rims, his special taillight covers, his new sound system, and oh yes, the Flowmaster exhaust muffler. You could hear the truck coming down the road a mile away. Cherise thought it was way too loud, which is the exact reason Terrell wanted it. He loved the way it sounded when he revved up the engine. Most men did.

Pastor Revenew was aware that Terrell had quit his job, and that he wasn't contributing to the household, so he was concerned as to where he was getting money to not just get a new truck, but to also make the expensive upgrades on it. Terrell told the pastor that he had gotten a re-enlistment bonus from the military, as well as a financial aid check, which allowed him to have money to do some of the things he wanted. The pastor asked Terrell if he had contributed any money to his household, and if so, how much?

Terrell became offended by all the questions Pastor Revenew was asking him. The pastor, noticing Terrell's frustration, explained to him that in order to even be allowed to minister in the church, he had to do what was right by his family. "God is a God of order, and He does not honor a man that doesn't take care of his own home. You can't expect to lead other people in ministry when you are not being a leader in your home," Pastor Revenew said sternly.

Terrell didn't like the way Pastor Revenew was handling him. He immediately got pissed. Cherise could remember his tone and the words he spoke towards the pastor. "You don't have anything to do with my house-hold, nor my money, so you can't tell me what to do with either. Just like you are the king of your castle, I am the king in mine, and I can do whatever I want. You're just a man like me, and personally, I think you're taking your role as pastor a little too far, trying to tell me how to run my house. If God is not pleased with the way I'm running things, He will tell me Himself."

Standing his ground, Pastor Revenew responded, "I am not trying to run your house, Brother Tillman, but you will not work on any auxiliary in this church, while you are blatantly disrespecting your wife and home." Pastor Revenew was the epitome of authority. He walked with authority. He talked with authority. He preached with authority. He prayed with authority, and whenever needed, just like today, he rebuked and chastised with authority. Even the devil knew when to flee because Charles Revenew just wasn't having it. Without a word, Terrell stood up and stormed out of the pastor's study, slamming the door behind him.

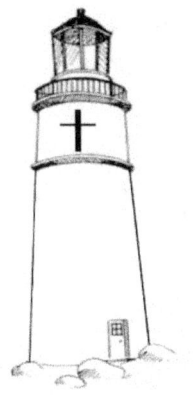

Chapter Three

One night during a casual discussion, Cherise shared with Terrell that God was calling her higher into ministry. What she wanted from him was support, and maybe a little understanding, but what she received was the complete opposite. He chastised her, and called her a liar, because God would have told him first.

"God doesn't work out of order. He always reveals things to the head first," he said with a boldness that would make a person who didn't know any better, believe what he was saying.

Cherise was so angry. She told him to kiss her you know what and to go you know where, all in the same breath. This time she didn't use "play-play" profanity. This time, she actually cussed him out.

Cherise's conduct must have come to a shock to Terrell, because he told her things were getting out of hand, and they needed to pray—immediately. This was totally out of character for her, but Terrell had really pressed her buttons. Trying to be submissive, she agreed, and they both fell on their knees. Terrell started…

"Father, we thank you for this day you have blessed us to see. We know you didn't have to do it, but because of your love, grace and mercy, you spared us, and we just wanna say thank you. We come before you tonight, as a couple, to pray for our marriage. You said in your word, where two or more are gathered together in your name, you would be in the midst, so we are coming before you, touching and agreeing that you would unify us as one.

"Now Lord, before we go any further with our prayer, we want to repent of any wrong that may have been done. I ask that you forgive Cherise for being disobedient and disrespectful to me, her husband." As Terrell continued praying, Cherise lifted her head and glared at him with an evil eye. "She needs to learn to submit to me because I have rule over her and not the other way around."

Cherise was burning up on the inside, and it took everything within her to not get up off the floor, and cuss him out some more. *I knew I shouldn't have allowed this fool to pray over me.*

While he prayed, she rebuked silently, *"Lord, I rebuke this prayer in the name of Jesus!"*

Terrell continued, "Lord, forgive her for not doing what I say, because even if she feels that I am wrong, she is to obey me like Sarah did Abraham, when he told her to lie and say she was his sister."

"I rebuke this prayer in the name of Jesus!"

"Lord, teach her, that she will have to learn to submit to me first, before you would even call her into ministry."

"I rebuke this prayer in the name of Jesus!"

"Teach her to obey those that have rule over her, and teach her to be quiet. Lord we bless you and all these blessings we ask in Jesus' name. Amen!"

"I rebuke this prayer in the name of Jesus!" She refused to say amen because there was nothing in this prayer that she was in agreement with.

The memories continued to crash around inside Cherise's head. She felt anxious as the ride finally approached its highest peak and made a sudden stop. Now she sat at the top of the steep hill, fearfully waiting with her eyes closed. She knew it would only be a matter of seconds before the train cart would tip forward. She tightly gripped the bars and held on for dear life, as she prepared herself for the big drop...

She thought about how Terrell quit his job without even consulting her. As the man of the house, she deemed this very selfish on his part. When she confronted him about it, he told her that he didn't have to discuss anything with her, because he was the head of the house, not her. He also told her that God created her to be a help meet, and that meant that she was supposed to help him in whatever area he felt he needed help in at the time, and right now, he needed her to pay all the bills until further notice.

Terrell had developed a bad habit of taking the Word of God, twisting it, and using it to benefit himself. And if there was one thing that made Cherise steaming mad, that was for someone to misuse the Word for their own benefit; especially Terrell.

On top of that, he had the nerve to tell her that she ought to be glad he at least considered her before making his decision to quit. He made sure that his monthly drill income was enough to cover his car note, car insurance, and any extra spending money he needed for himself; anything else, she could take care of since she made the most money. This was the real truth behind why he didn't want to help her, and this was his way of punishing her for making more money than him.

Cherise was thankful for her great paying job. She was a team leader at one of the major phone companies that provided support and customer service to customers throughout the United States. She was nowhere near rich, but the money she made allowed her to take care of all of her and the girls' needs, and most of their wants. She constantly told herself that although she didn't know it, God knew just what she would be dealing with at this moment in her life, and that is why He blessed her with such a great job. She really didn't have to rely on Terrell for much of anything, but that didn't give him an excuse to abandon his responsibilities of being a husband or a father.

Speaking of a car note—it's funny how he didn't have any money to help pay bills, but all of a sudden, out of nowhere one day, he comes home driving a brand new, shiny blue, Dodge Ram 1500. Now if that wasn't a slap in the face! Cherise took a deep breath at the memory and her thoughts continued…

Cherise always depended on Terrell to keep the fluids checked in her car, so when it ran hot due to no oil, she was at a loss for words. Then when she called him to pick her up from where she was stranded on the side of a less traveled road, he told her that she would have to wait until he finished eating and took a shower. Did he not care? Apparently not.

Thank God for roadside assistance. They seemed to care more about her situation than her own husband. They arrived rather quickly too, but with two husky gentleman riding in the truck, they didn't have the room for Cherise and the kids to catch a ride. They did, however, offer to wait until someone came to her aide. Out of all days, no one she called was available. Her father was the last person she wanted to call, but being stranded in the hot sun, with kids, waiting on Terrell, was the last place she wanted to be.

The cost to have the Chrysler Sebring repaired was more than what she could afford. She would either have to apply for a loan, and pay that bill along with the already existing car payment, or see about getting another car. Cherise had favor at the same dealership where she purchased her first car, and was able to trade in the Sebring for a new Grand Cherokee Jeep. She still owed a significant amount on the car, and was now considered to be upside down.

To help offset the cost, she asked Terrell to cosign for her. Since he wouldn't help her with any of the bills, at least if he signed, she could get a better interest rate on financing. Without even thinking about it, he answered her flat out— NO. He told her that he didn't want to take a chance on her messing up his good credit and that he didn't want to be tied to any loans with her. This resulted in her monthly car payments increasing from $427 per month, to $687. It was in that instant that Cherise realized she was completely on her own, and from this moment forward, she would never ask anything of Terrell again.

Being without a car was not an option. She had to do what she had to do, which is why she ended up with the Sebring in the first place. She originally had a Saturn that Terrell had purchased for her. Not that he made the payments, he just signed for it. All because his signature was on the loan, he felt that he could control her going and coming. When she didn't do things as he wanted her to, which was hardly ever, he would detach the wires from the battery so that she would be stranded and could not leave the house in "his" car. She'd warned him last time—should he disable anything else on the car again, she would relinquish complete ownership of it to him. She would no longer pay for transportation that she couldn't have access to at all time.

About a month later, Alysa was trying to play a game on the computer, and pop-ups of what Alysa would call, "nakey boo boos"—men and women, flashed on the screen. Cherise was furious! How many more times did she have to tell Terrell about going to those filthy sites? She could care less about what he was doing, but her responsibility was to shield her kids from such things. So if that meant blocking him off the computer, then that's just what she would do.

Later that night when Terrell couldn't log onto the computer, he confronted Cherise. She simply told him what happened and that he would need to get his own computer to do that kind of foolery on. After a few choice words, he exited the bedroom where he had interrupted Cherise praying, and went back into the living room and disassembled the computer desk. He told her that—if he couldn't use the computer, then she needed to put together her own computer desk. He would not allow her to benefit from his hard work. You see, all this was because he put the desk together the first time.

Cherise went to bed and figured everything was over and done with, until she woke up the next morning running late for work. Terrell had deliberately turned off her alarm on the dual alarm clock they shared. He earned the clock as a gift from his previous job before he resigned. His attitude was—since it was his clock, if he couldn't use her computer, she couldn't use his clock.

After loading Alysa in the car, she rushed to the driver's side. When she turned the key in the ignition, the car would not start. Cherise couldn't believe it; Terrell had done it again. She decided that she wouldn't even give him the satisfaction of asking him to fix the car so she could go to work—she just called in for the day. As of that day, she could not afford to play games with him when it came to her job. Especially, since it was her only means of support.

When Terrell came home later that evening, he found a new Chrysler Sebring sitting in the driveway. This was one car he couldn't control or take anything apart on. He was mad, but as far as Cherise was concerned, it served him right.

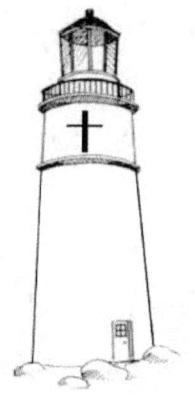

Chapter Four

Boy was this ride doing a number on Cherise. All the ups and downs, jerks and pulls, and loops and curves were really making her sick to her stomach. As much as she wanted to get off, she was in too deep.

The bath water had lost its sting and was no longer giving her the relaxing sensation she desired. So with tears streaming down her face, she sat up and turned on the hot water to heat the bath back up to a more satisfying temperature. After lying back down with her body submerged under the water, her thoughts continued...

She often wondered why and how God allowed Terrell to do some, no, all of the crazy things he did, especially since he claimed to be a minister and all. She couldn't even think the wrong things sometimes, before God would chastise her. So, why could Terrell get away with murder? Well, maybe murder was a little extreme, but he sure got away with some low-down dirty things.

Like the time when Cherise's cell phone rang at two o'clock in the morning. She was asleep and didn't even know it had gone off, but Terrell heard it, and picked it up and went through it to see who had called her. Since he didn't recognize the number, he woke Cherise up and questioned her about it.

When Cherise looked at the phone, she didn't recognize the number and told him it was probably a wrong number. Terrell was not satisfied with her response, and told her he was not buying it, and then demanded she call the number back. When Cherise refused, he called the number back himself. Cherise recalled the conversation between Terrell and the person on the other end of the phone...

"Hey, did someone just call this number?" Terrell asked.

"Yeah man, my bad." The voice of the man was innocent, and friendly. "I did just dial a wrong number by mistake. I didn't realize I had dialed the wrong number until the voicemail came on. I'm sorry if I woke you."

"Well, this phone actually belongs to my wife, Cherise. Do you know her?"

"Naw man, I don't know anyone by that name. I didn't mean any harm, and I'm sorry if I've caused any problems, but it was honestly a mistake."

"No problem."

When Terrell hung up the call, he looked at Cherise and threatened, "If I ever find out that you are messing around with anybody, I promise you, I'ma kill you."

This was not the first time Terrell had threatened Cherise, and she was pretty certain, it wouldn't be the last. Anytime they got into a real heated argument, he conveniently had to do something with his gun. He always made it seem like he was just cleaning it, or just doing regular maintenance on it, but Cherise knew that it was a scare tactic. She really didn't know if he was capable of carrying out his threats, but living with him had become extremely uncomfortable, and she really just wanted a way out.

As the thriller ride was coming to an end, she thought about the day Terrell came home and asked her to go with him to the bank to remove her name off his account. He had accepted a special assignment from the military, where he would serve as security at one of the military bases for a year. This required him to live away from home during that time, but he could come home on his days off. This also required him to be activated as full-time military, getting full-time pay, and benefits.

"I'm not taking my name off any bank account. What if an emergency comes up, or what if I need some money for the kids?" Cherise asked.

"You can contact the Red Cross, and they will get in contact with me. I just don't want you having access to my money while I'm away. Too many wives have already stolen other soldier's money while they were away, and when they came home, they didn't have anything. I need you to do this so that I can have a peace of mind." Terrell explained.

"All these years, as long as I was bringing in the most money, it was okay for us to share accounts, but now that you are getting ready to come into some money, you want me to take my name off of your account?" she asked in disbelief. "You must be crazy!"

"Fine. You don't have to do it, I'll just get a new account," he responded.

That's exactly what he did. Since he couldn't close their joint account without her signature, he opened a new account where he was the only one that had access to it. He changed all his direct deposit information with the military, and all of his money went into the new account. He told Cherise that he would give her what he felt she needed each month to get by, especially since she already had a good job, making good money.

Terrell's knavery was obvious when it came to matters of his income. He told Cherise he was only making $2500 per month, but thanks to her friend and co-worker Sybill, whose husband was also in the military, she found out that Terrell was banking close to $4000 per month due to his high ranking, and the extra allowances he received from being married, and having a home.

Sybill Evans was one of Cherise's closest friends, besides Sasha Hayes. They all started work on the same day, and had become extremely close throughout the years. Sasha was a short lil thang, who they always picked on about her height. I don't think she was even five feet tall.

Although small, sista girl was a bad mamma jamma. She was always dressed to kill and her hairdos were always tight. The best one yet was the Minnie Bow. All her hair was pulled into a ponytail, designed into a perfect bow tie on the top of her head. She would be known as Minnie, Mickey Mouse's girl for a long time coming. Sasha was saved as well, so, she was always the voice of reason, and she related more to Cherise when it came to spiritual things.

Now Sybill, on the other hand, was a hot mess. She had the perfect name. She was beautiful like the actress, and former model, Cybill Shepherd, who starred in the 1985 television series, *Moonlighting,* and she was as crazy as, Sybil Isabel Dorsett— the movie about a young woman who was vexed with at least sixteen personalities.

Sybill had a big heart, and was as sweet as could be. If she loved you, you knew it, and if she hated you, you knew it. She was very outspoken, and would tell you off in a minute. It was nothing for her to "rip someone a new butthole" as she would call it. If you started it, she was sure to finish it. Her motto was—don't start none, won't be none.

Sasha would always encourage Cherise when it came to her marriage. Sybill would encourage her too—encourage her to leave, encourage her to cut Terrell up, encourage her to burn him up in a scorching bed, and encourage her to pick up something and knock him out. She didn't like the way Terrell was treating her friend, and if she could, she would do something to him.

Cherise smiled when she thought about her two girlfriends. There was nothing she wouldn't do for them, and vice versa. No matter what, they always had each other's backs. She knew, without a shadow of a doubt, that if she called, they would come running. She had two fighters on her team. One that would fight in the Spirit, and one that would just straight up fight. You can't beat that if you tried.

Her thoughts immediately reverted back to Terrell. If hiding the money wasn't bad enough, about a month after he'd left, Cherise received a letter from the military, advising her that Terrell's beneficiary had been changed. According to the letter, they couldn't advise her as to whom the new beneficiary was, but by law, they had to inform her of the change. When she confronted him about the letter, he advised her that he changed it to his mom, because he felt that if anything happened to him while he was on active duty, he didn't want her getting rich off his money, living it up with another man.

Thank God this adventure was finally over. Cherise had been in the bathroom for a little more than an hour, and after a good cry and a little talk with Jesus, she felt refreshed and revived. After dinner, she joined Alyson and Alysa in their room to watch a few episodes of the *That's So Raven* marathon. The girls loved it when their mommy came in their room and watched TV with them. They called it, "girl time." Cherise called it, "getting away from Terrell", however, she loved the teen comedy just as much as the kids.

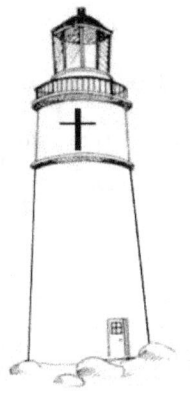

Chapter Five

Cherise fell on her knees and bent over the toilet vomiting and crying uncontrollably. The sexual encounter she had just experienced with Terrell was sickening. Everything about him literally made her sick to her stomach. His voice, his touch, his kiss, and to have him lying on top of her was just torture. However, this time didn't last as long as others because she forced him to hurry up. She wouldn't deny him, but she was sure to make him feel just as uncomfortable as she was.

She'd stayed up late and had fallen asleep on the sofa, as she always did as a means to avoid Terrell, and to keep him from bothering her. When she awoke around 2 a.m., she figured it was safe to go to bed. *Surely, he should be good and asleep by now,* she thought. As soon as she had positioned herself comfortably on her right side, with her back facing Terrell, she felt his hand rubbing on her hip. *Darn it! I should have stayed on the sofa a little longer.* She rolled her eyes as soon as he started struggling with trying to remove her pajama pants and underwear.

She decided against putting up a fight because it only prolonged the time. All she wanted was for this ordeal to hurry up and be over with. She turned over on her back, and rested her feet flat on the bed, with her knees up. Without hesitation, she lifted her bottom off the mattress to allow easy removal of her clothes.

Terrell wasted no time getting on top of her, and as soon as he entered her, tears began flowing down her face. *Jesus, Jesus, Jesus…*Cherise silently called. When Terrell tried to kiss her, she pressed her lips together tightly, and turned her head away. She just couldn't stomach him sticking his tongue in her mouth—morning breath or not.

Terrell ignored her resistance, and tried to kiss her a second time, but this time Cherise exploded. "I said NO! So if you want some, you better quit wasting time and hurry up. As a matter of fact, you got two minutes to get finished."

"Two minutes?" Terrell questioned. "Are you serious?"

"You heard me," Cherise uttered with a despicable frown her face.

"Maaaaaaan, you're tripping."

"And you got one minute and fifty seconds, so I suggest you hurry up," she said matter-of-factly, and continued counting down in her head.

"Are you seriously counting?" Terrell asked in disbelief.

"One minute and forty-five seconds."

Terrell realized Cherise was not joking, and decided not to waste any more time talking; he had to get busy. The next sixty seconds felt like sixty minutes to Cherise. Believe it or not, she was still counting down in her head. She was not giving him an extra second to pound on her.

For the most part, Cherise was submissive to her husband. There was nothing he did so great to deserve it, but she tried to honor God's Word. Anytime she wanted to be insubordinate, she remembered Ephesians 5:22, "Wives, submit yourselves unto your own husbands as unto the Lord." The words, "as unto the Lord" was the key to her sanity. She constantly told herself that whatever she did for Terrell was not really for him. She convinced herself that Terrell was not even a factor in the equation. It was just her and God. Everything she did was, "as unto the Lord." From cooking, to cleaning, to doing his laundry was "as unto the Lord." Even though Terrell wasn't doing his part as a husband and he definitely was not loving her as Christ loved the church, and gave Himself for it, she still did her part—all of it, "as unto the Lord." This way of thinking helped her to not feel used; however, she just couldn't see how allowing Terrell to keep pleasuring himself with her was, "as unto the Lord." Not with the way she felt afterwards.

Cherise was now at the thirty second mark, and to ensure Terrell knew exactly how much time he had left, she began counting out loud. "Thirty, twenty-nine, twenty-eight..."

Almost out of breath, Terrell panted, "Man.... quit......that....... shhh..."

"Twenty-five, twenty-four, twenty-three......."

"Cherise! Stop it!" he pleaded. Terrell had to do some serious concentrating, and Cherise was making it extremely hard, with her annoying countdown. "Please shut up!" he begged, with a slightly increased voice.

Ignoring his outburst, "Eighteen, seventeen, sixteen…"

Terrell was sweating profusely, and was doing all he could to finish before the timer reached zero. He would never let her know it, but Cherise had him in a very uncomfortable position.

His ego had taken a low blow, below the belt, and just as she wished, he was not getting any pleasure out of this at all.

"Five, four, three, two, one." Cherise was relieved. "Time's up! Get up!" She positioned her hands, one on each shoulder and gave him a push that indicated she wanted to get up.

Terrell felt like his heart was about to jump out of his chest. He made it to the finish line, but he didn't feel like a champion; more like a loser. He rolled off of Cherise onto his back, and struggled to catch his breath. Cherise immediately rushed to the bathroom, and closed the door.

Every time she submitted sexually "as unto the Lord", she felt as if she had been raped. After her attacker had taken what he wanted from her, she was left alone, wounded, and in indescribable pain. She felt nasty, filthy, and disgusting. A normal shower and scrub was never enough to wash away the residue that was left behind. Now she lay in the bathroom, stripped before God crying, begging Him to deliver her from such pain. Was this what submitting "as unto the Lord" was supposed to feel like?

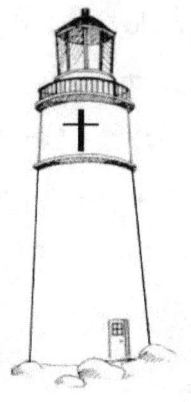

Chapter Six

G ood Morning, Cherise!" Mario greeted as he handed her a stack of mail. "You look nice today."

Smiling, she responded, "Thank you, Mario." She took the envelopes. "How are you today?"

"I'm good. What about you?"

"I'm fine."

Jokingly, but yet serious, Mario teased, "I can see that, but how are you doing?" He really had a thing for Cherise.

Trying not to blush, she laughed, "Ok, Ok, you got me, but you know what I meant."

They both shared a tender laugh, and for a brief moment, an intimate stare in each other's eyes. Mario bit his bottom lip, and shook his head before walking away. They both wanted each other, but didn't want to eat of the forbidden fruit.

Mario worked at the telephone company, and was responsible for the mass incoming and outgoing mail for the entire building. The company consisted of approximately three-hundred employees, the vast majority being women. Many of the ladies flirted with him on a daily basis, but none of them fazed him like Cherise. She was different, and didn't appear to be easy like the rest of them. To him, she was beautiful, classy, sexy, and smart. Even if she didn't have any mail for the day, he went out of his way to see her, even if it was from afar.

Mario knew that Cherise was married by the wedding ring she sported, but he couldn't deny the strong attraction he had for her either. If the truth be told, she was just as attracted to him, but this was her little secret that she wouldn't—no couldn't—tell anyone about.

There was no way she could tell anybody that she had a secret crush on the mailroom guy. And there was absolutely no way she could tell anybody that—just as much as Mario went out of his way to see her every day, just to tell her how nice she looked—that she needed to see him, just to hear those words. Those words became a lifeline for her. Those words made her feel beautiful, and special. Those words became so addictive, that she went home every evening, planning the perfect outfit that would guarantee her, her next compliment. Just like a crack-head, she had to have it.

Not that Cherise had self-esteem issues or anything like that, because she didn't. She spoke daily affirmations and confessions over herself daily. She was very confident, but she couldn't deny that she loved the extra attention she was getting from another man. Terrell had stopped giving her compliments years ago. He was not caring, loving, or affectionate anymore, so the interest of another man was exciting to her.

They had exchanged numbers months ago when she invited him to come to church for one of the many special programs New Harvest was known for having. Somehow, what started out as a simple contact for purposes of getting directions to the church, ending up being a means to have intense daily conversations. They only spoke on the phone when she was alone, but they would text all throughout the day, even if Terrell was around. His presence made the conversations even better, because it seemed like they were sneaking, and that gave Cherise a rush.

As hard as Mario tried to respect the fact that Cherise was another man's wife, he was falling fast. The more they communicated, the more he wanted to be with her. They had discussed meeting up several times, but Cherise just couldn't take that chance. She enjoyed the wonderful compliments, the intense conversations, and a little flirting every now and then, but she had no intention of actually becoming intimate with him—if she could help it.

They were already playing with fire, but sleeping together would be more like jumping directly in it. This thing was scary, and Cherise feared the results of the morning after. Either Mario would not be good in bed, then she would have to kick herself for sinning and have to deal with the guilt of it. Or, he could actually be so good, that she would lose her mind, and want to give up everything, just to be with him. Either way, the risk was too great, and Cherise didn't want to gamble with it.

As hard as she tried to stay faithful to Terrell, "as unto the Lord", she found herself in bed being pleasured by another man. That night, she enjoyed the gentle touch of warm hands stroking her face, and warm tender kisses on her neck. Passion-filled hands caressed her breasts; not too hard, and not too soft, but just the way she liked it. The kisses trailed from her neck to her breasts. She trembled, as her body desired more, but that was as far as it went that night.

A few days later, Cherise realized that this thing, whatever it was, had really gotten out of control, when she allowed her lover to fondle her, while standing at the back of her jeep. The idea of being seen while making out, added more excitement to this sinful escapade. He stood behind her, and kissed the back of her neck. He knew just what to do to make her body hunger for him. He raised her skirt with his left hand, as he massaged her right breast with his right one. He placed his left hand in her panties, and he stroked her until she burned with desire. With the trunk of the jeep opened, he picked her up, and positioned her on her knees. She could hardly wait to feel him. He was just about to make contact, when Cherise heard someone calling her name.

"Cherise. Cherise." Terrell's voice was getting louder. "What's wrong with you?" he asked.

She tried to respond, but the grip he had on her shoulder scared her. He shook her with a moderate force, until she responded. She couldn't explain the mixture of emotions she was feeling. She was scared, embarrassed, ashamed, confused, guilty, and most of all, she was relieved. As much as she despised Terrell, she was happy that he'd caught her at the moment he did. Although she was extremely close to it, he had just prevented her from crossing the line; again. After she gathered her thoughts, she finally spoke, "I...I was having a bad nightmare."

Terrell wasn't interested in her dreams; he just wanted her to stop moving so much in the bed. All of her tossing and turning kept interrupting his night's rest. Now that he knew she was awake, he attempted to go back to sleep. Cherise, on the other hand, was scared to go back to sleep. She had been having these nightmares all week, and although she was dreaming, these episodes were real. She could feel every kiss, every touch, and every stroke in her natural flesh. Someone or something was making real love to her as she slept, and one thing she knew for sure, it wasn't her husband. Whatever it was, it had Mario's face.

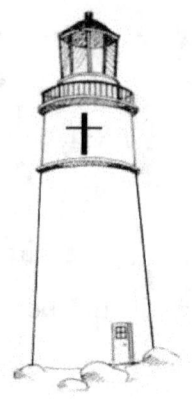

Chapter Seven

Cherise's spirit was heavy. She knew how to pray, but this morning, she needed to be prayed for. After dropping the girls off at school and daycare, she called Pastor Revenew.

"Good Morning," he answered joyfully.

"Good Morning, Pastor." Her tone was dry. "I'm sorry for calling so early, but I really need you to pray for me." She tried, but she was unsuccessful in her attempt to hold back her tears.

"What's wrong, daughter?"

"Something is attacking me in my dreams. It's actually attempting to make love to me. Although, I'm asleep, I feel him. I feel everything he does to me. I can't explain it, but it's like I'm sleep, but I'm awake at the same time. Once I'm fully conscious, I realize that it was a dream, but there's a feeling of guilt that is left with me. Every time it happens, I feel like I've sinned. I need these dreams to stop, because I'm afraid of what might happen if we go all the way." Cherise wept like a helpless little girl.

Pastor Revenew felt her pain. He knew what she was telling him was indeed real. He had never experienced it personally, but had heard of it before. He remembered that he had some books in his study that talked about these types of spirits. He was actually already in the study reading the newspaper before Cherise had called, which made it easy for him to look through the neatly organized rows of books.

"Cherise, it's okay." He sympathized with her cry. "I believe everything you're telling me."

Shocked by his response, "You do?"

"Yes! So stop thinking that you're crazy, because you're not." He pulled a book from his bookshelf, and studied the index to find what he was looking for. Upon flipping the pages of the book, he continued, "You're dealing with a spirit called incubus. This spirit seeks to have sex with people while they are asleep. Incubus is the name of the spirit that tries to sleep with women, and succubus is the name of the one that tries to sleep with men."

Cherise was speechless by the words that were coming from Pastor Revenew's lips. It was indeed, times like these that made her appreciate her pastor and the wisdom and knowledge he possessed. She sat listening to him, paying very close attention to all he had to say.

"This spirit has the ability to change its form to appear as a man, or even someone you actually know. They manifest themselves in your subconscious, which allows you to experience all the stimulation, and every feeling that you would normally feel during sexual contact with a real person. These spirits are very skilled in making a person to feel ecstasy, so in most cases, the person that this is happening to actually enjoys the pleasure they are feeling. It is not until they wake up that they realize something strange has happened. Although it may seem strange, what you were experiencing is very real."

Everything that Pastor Revenew had just described was exactly what she had experienced. For a minute there, she thought she was actually going crazy. Now she understood why Mario was the one in her dreams, however, she would never tell Pastor Revenew about Mario.

As if he was reading her mind, Pastor Revenew said concernedly, "Cherise, these spirits don't just appear, but in most cases, have to have an invitation. I'm not sure what's going on in your life, but I strongly suggest you search within yourself, and ask God to show you any doors that you may have allowed to open for these spirits to enter. For some, these doors could be rape or molestation; things beyond their control. For others, it could be things like fornication, adultery, pornography, and something as simple as flirting, or having sexual desires for someone other than your spouse, and so on.

"It is a good thing you called. Most people, because they don't understand it, or can't even explain it, remain silent and never tell anyone. It's possible that they could be a little embarrassed too, and I can only imagine it must be hard to tell somebody something like this. Nevertheless, I'm glad you called."

Cherise felt relieved. "Me too, Pastor. I feel so much better."

"Good." Pastor Revenew smiled. He gave her a few more words of encouragement, and ended the call in prayer.

Cherise spent the whole day at work ruminating on the information and counsel Pastor Revenew had given her. She couldn't tell the pastor, but she knew that she had opened the door for this spirit to come in. She was determined, with the Lord's help, to close that door, and put a deadbolt lock on it.

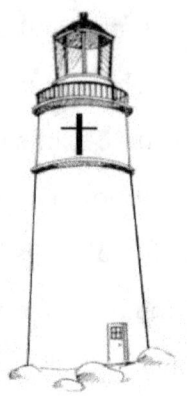

Chapter Eight

Tuesday night Bible study ran a little longer than normal. Terrell didn't attend now that Cherise had been licensed as a minister, and was given the responsibility of teaching the adult class. After the service, one of the sisters in the church requested to speak with Cherise before leaving to go home.

Cherise had also been appointed as president over the women's auxiliary, so she got this kind of attention a lot. She was highly respected by everyone in the church, but the women of New Harvest adored her, and likewise, she had a special love for them. Cherise spoke with the lady for about thirty minutes, prayed with her, and hugged and kissed the woman goodbye. After both ladies were safely in their cars, she drove to her mother's house to get the girls.

After the sister had requested to speak with Cherise, her mom decided to take the girls home with her to get them prepared for bed. That would be one less thing Cherise would have to do when she got home. After picking up the girls, and getting them settled in bed, she went to her room and started preparing for a bath.

Terrell startled her when he entered the room. She didn't know he was home since his truck wasn't in the front yard as usual. She later found out that he had parked it in the back of the house, and was hiding in the den until she came home. This was out of the norm, so she wouldn't have thought to look for it back there.

"Oooh," she responded to his presence with a jump. Placing her right hand on the left side of her chest, she announced, "God, you scared me!"

"I bet I did. Where have you been?" he asked in an angry tone.

"At church," she quickly answered.

"I called the church, and no one answered. I also called your phone too, so where have you been?"

"I told you I've been at church. Bible study ended a little late and one of the members wanted to speak with me afterwards."

"Who? Ronald?"

Trying to keep her cool. "No. One of the ladies at the church."

Terrell didn't believe her. He grabbed her by the arm and pushed her on the bed.

"Let go of me!" she yelled. "What are you doing?"

"I'm checking to see if you've been messing around," he said as he tussled to pin her down.

Cherise wrestled with him to the best of her ability, to keep him from ripping off her clothes, but his strength was too much for her to handle. She finally gave up her fight, and lay dorsal and helpless on the bed while Terrell removed her panties and smelled them. As if that wasn't enough, he forced her to open her legs, and began to examine her like he had a degree in gynecology.

Never in a million years had Cherise felt so violated, and to think, by her own husband. He must have been turned on by the explicit scene before him, because after he finished his inspection, he proceeded to have forceful sex with her.

Anger and rage began to fill Cherise's heart. She tried her best to never get angry because the thoughts she would have would always be deadly. Like right now, as Terrell lay on top of her, she was looking at a pair of scissors on the dresser, and could visualize herself cutting off his genitals. The scriptures opened up before her eyes, and she envisioned herself standing in Cain's place. She heard the warning loud and clear—sin was lying at the door, and she would have to choose to not fall prey and succumb to it. She knew that she was close to doing something she might regret later.

Once Terrell was finished, he rolled off of her onto his back. He was sleep within minutes. Cherise ran to her only sanctuary in the house to cry and pray. She prayed for her sanity. She prayed for strength, not to kill Terrell in his sleep. She prayed for God to help relieve her of the bitterness that was growing inside of her. She prayed for God to release her out of this marriage.

As she walked out of the bathroom, Cherise stood in front of the mirror and watched Terrell as he slept, as if he had no worries. When she thought about what he had just done to her, and everything he had put her through, tears began to flow down her face. Her heart was heavy, and she dreaded getting in the bed to lie beside that man in the mirror. He was not her husband, and he was definitely not her friend. She grabbed the cross on her neck with her right hand, and prayed for protection, as she prepared to sleep with the enemy.

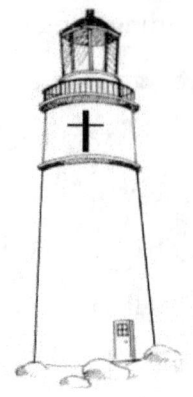

Chapter Nine

Cherise could hardly get out of bed the next morning. Her body was sore from all that wrestling she did with Terrell the night before. With Terrell having morning and evening classes, she decided to take advantage of the day, and requested a vacation day from work. She wasn't worried about him coming home for lunch or anything, because the school was at least thirty minutes away—too far to leave, come home, and go back.

Determined to find a way of escape, Cherise pulled out her Bible, and began diligently seeking for scriptures that would justify her leaving her husband. There was no way she could stay with Terrell after last night. Just the mere sight of him disgusted her.

After hours upon hours of reading scripture after scripture and commentary notes, Cherise got madder. Nothing she read supported her situation. There were many scriptures that talked about—if a spouse leaves, but that was the problem— Terrell wasn't leaving. He wasn't going anywhere because, he had it all. He was having his cake, and eating it too. He didn't have to pay any bills, he always had food to eat, clean clothes, and all his basic needs were being met—even his sexual needs. He would be a fool to leave an arrangement like this.

This may have been the perfect life for him, but not for Cherise. She was so desperate for a way out, that she pulled the Gideon card. She just couldn't believe that God wanted her to endure all of the things she was dealing with in the marriage any longer. So, unto the Lord she said, "Lord, I have tried. I really don't want to continue in this situation. I am tired of going to church, leading praise and worship, teaching Bible study, preaching, and after service—coming home to hell. I don't want to stay, but I don't want to displease you."

Cherise was planning to file for a divorce, but wanted a sign from God to confirm that she was doing the right thing. Desperately she bargained, "In the Bible, when Gideon needed a sign for confirmation, you answered. So today, I ask for a sign from you. You know what I am planning to do, but if this is against your will, I ask that you please not allow Terrell to come home starting with me today. If he comes home and starts an argument for no reason, I'm going to accept this as your permission to file for a divorce. If he comes home, and doesn't start anything with me, I will consider this as your sign to stay put, and I will not file."

Cherise checked the time and realized that it was soon time for Terrell to be coming home from school. She decided to take a wash and put on some clothes before going to get the girls. After she returned home, she cooked dinner and helped Alyson with her homework, while Alysa watched *Dora* on the TV. Shortly after, she heard the earsplitting sounds of the thunderous engine, as it turned on the street. It was time to see which way God wanted her to go.

Alysa was waiting on Terrell to come in the house. She too, had learned the sound of her daddy's truck. As he entered, Alysa ran to him with excitement. He welcomed her with a smile and opened arms. He picked her up, kissed her, and put her back on the floor. As he made his way through the house, he spoke to both Alyson and Cherise. He asked Alyson about her day, and proceeded to the bathroom to take a shower.

Cherise never understood why he always needed to shower when he came home, since he didn't work. She suspected he was having an affair, but she didn't have any proof. Shoot, Cherise was so desperate for a way out; she had once prayed that he would cheat. She had to soon repent for wishing sin on someone's life—even if it was Terrell.

After showering, Terrell was on his way to the kitchen, but stopped to answer the phone.

"Hello."

"Hey Bro. Tillman. How you doing?"

"Just fine. Just fine. How 'bout you?"

"Oh, I'm good. I was just calling to find out what time was the "Joy Night" program this Saturday?"

Joy Night was one of those many programs The Harvest (the nickname many of the members used when referring to the church) would have from time to time. It really wasn't any different than any other service, but because this was actually a fundraiser the Hospitality Ministry of the church was sponsoring, someone dressed it up with a title. There was still singing, shouting and preaching, however, Joy Night consisted of other surrounding churches fellowshipping together, and all the monies raised in offerings were used toward the Pastor Appreciation Day.

"I think it's at seven o'clock, but let me let you talk to Cherise about it, since she helps with all that, okay?"

"Okay. Sure."

Cherise was watching her favorite show, *The Gilmore Girls*, when Terrell passed her the phone. "Here, your boyfriend is on the phone," he said in a tone which was supposed to be a whisper, but could have been heard by the party on the other end had not his hand been over the mouthpiece.

Cherise took the phone, wondering who was on the other end. Puzzled she answered, "Hello."

"Heeeey, Sis. Cherise. How you doing?"

Rolling her eyes at Terrell, she responded to the caller, "Oh—Hi Bro. Dukes. How are you?"

"I'm doing pretty good. I was just wondering what time is the program on Saturday night?"

"Oh, that's not a problem. It's at six. Hopefully we won't be in there too long, but you know how it is when the Spirit starts moving."

"That's okay with me. How are the girls?"

Ronald loved to talk. Without any family in the area, he seized every opportunity to communicate. Cherise didn't mind conversing, but not while her show was on. Three commercials had run, so she knew the episode would be back on in just a minute.

"The girls are fine. I'm getting ready to prepare them for their baths in a few," she said rushing him off the phone.

"Well okay then. I'll let you go. That's all I really wanted—so I'll just see y'all on Saturday."

"Alright, Bro. Dukes. You have a good night." Cherise quickly hung up the phone before he could respond.

"I knew you were messing with that drunk," Terrell uttered.

"Terrell, please don't start. I am not in the mood to argue with you about something so stupid. Ronald didn't call here and ask for me, you pushed him off on me. You could have just asked me for the time." Annoyed, she further stated, "As a matter of fact, he wouldn't even have our number if you hadn't given it to him."

"Whatever—I'm sure he knew what time the program was. He was probably calling to give you some type of booty call code, so y'all could meet up. You were probably with him today, since you didn't go to work."

Cherise decided not to continue arguing with Terrell, because God had given her the sign she prayed for—and tomorrow, she was filing for a divorce.

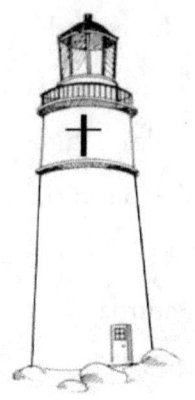

Chapter Ten

That night, Cherise could not sleep at all. She had rehearsed the plan in her mind a thousand times. She felt a little sad, because she knew that her decision would have a major effect on her children. Hopefully, Terrell would be man enough to still be a father, even if he wasn't in the home.

The next morning, Cherise did everything as usual. She got the kids ready for school, and dressed as if she was going to work. She left home at the normal time, but instead of going to work, she paid a visit to the office of Michelle Montgomery, Esq.

"Good Morning." The attractive, young receptionist greeted. "May I help you?"

"Yes. My name is Cherise Tillman, and I'm interested in filing for a divorce."

"Do you have an appointment, Mrs. Tillman?"

"No, I'm sorry. This was sort of a last minute decision," Cherise explained.

"That's not a problem. Ms. Montgomery's first appointment is not until later this morning, so I'm sure she will be able to speak with you," the receptionist assured. "Give me one moment to let her know you're here." Gesturing to the black leather seats, she informed, "Have a seat and I'll be right back."

"Thanks!"

Cherise took the seat offered by the young lady and tried to relax. She was nervous, but at the same time, she was excited. She felt like this was another sign—God was actually in favor of what she was about to do.

After a few minutes, the young lady returned. "Excuse me Mrs. Tillman," she interrupted Cherise's thoughts. "Mrs. Montgomery will be a few minutes—she's on a call with a client." Cherise looked up at the woman and smiled. She was very pleased at the professionalism and service she was getting thus far.

No more than ten minutes later, the attorney walked out, introduced herself, and invited Cherise into her office. She aimed her right hand at the burgundy leather chair sitting in front of her desk. "Have a seat," she offered.

After Cherise was seated, Attorney Montgomery inquired, "How may I help you?"

"Um… I'm interested in filing for a divorce."

"Okay. On what grounds will you be filing?"

Although she suspected it, she never had any proof that Terrell was unfaithful, so, she couldn't use that as an excuse. She could have used, Cruel and Abusive Treatment, among other things, but she didn't want to deal with having to prove fault on his behalf. She just wanted to get this over as quickly as possible, and with less fight as possible. At the end of the day, she just wanted out.

"Irreconcilable Differences," Cherise chose.

"Okay. Are there any children from the marriage?"

"Um, yes—I have two, but only one with my husband."

"I understand. However, legally, he is only responsible for the one that you and he have together."

"I understand."

"What about property, or anything like that? How will everything be split between the two of you?"

"I'm not sure about that. We really don't have anything to split. He has his car, I have mine, and we are currently renting a house."

"I see. Well, it seems like it will be pretty simple, should you decide to go through with the divorce, and provided your spouse does not choose to contest." Curiously, she asked, "Do you know if it will be contested or uncontested?"

Cherise already knew that Terrell wasn't going down without a fight. "I hope uncontested, but if I know Terrell, it will probably be contested—just because."

"Well, that will determine the final cost. If it's uncontested, it will cost you approximately $600. We can probably get the process completed within about two months, and that's because, in the state of Georgia, anyone that gets a divorce with kids, has to attend a class. In the case your husband does contest the divorce, we will have to go before a judge, and the process time can really vary. This of course, will cost you around $2000."

"Wow. That really is a big difference."

"That it is. So, if both parties can come to a mutual agreement about everything, uncontested is definitely the best way to go."

"I see."

The attorney quickly scanned her paper to make sure she didn't miss anything. "Looks like that's pretty much it, Mrs. Tillman. Today's consultation is free, so if you decide that you would like to file, I will be more than happy to represent you."

Cherise didn't waste any time on deciding whether to go forward or not—she was just waiting for the signal to change to "go". "I'm actually ready to file today."

Filing for the divorce was fairly easy, but the dilemma was getting Terrell out of the house. Attorney Montgomery advised Cherise, that the law prevented them from making him leave the home without a restraining order. However, if she felt threatened by him, they could get one processed today.

This was perfect! Terrell had pulled that gun out on her, more times than she could remember—and let's not forget about the time he had actually, verbally threatened her, when someone had mistakenly called her phone. Although she didn't want to use this as grounds for the divorce, she would definitely take advantage of this opportunity to remove him out of her space.

Now that everything was put into motion, she felt overwhelmed, scared even. She had no idea how Terrell was going to react, so, she packed up enough clothes for her and the girls, and went to stay with her dad for a few days. There, she felt safe, and knew she didn't have to worry about anybody bothering her.

You had to be a ridiculously bold person to come to Dellwood Curry's house acting crazy. Her father was quite foolish himself, and ever since she was a little girl, she could remember her father saying, "I'll kill a rock, and put a piece of iron in the hospital about mine." That Dellwood Curry was a bad man, or at least, that's the impression he gave Cherise. Whether he could accomplish such outrageous tasks or not was clearly obvious, however, the mere thought that he could, made her feel safe.

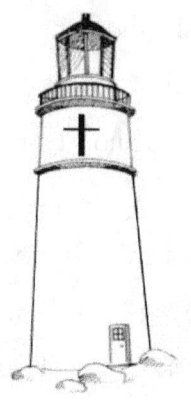

Chapter Eleven

The loud knock on the door startled Terrell. He was just finishing up his shower, but hadn't yet dried off. The knocks were becoming more demanding, and he wondered who it could be. He wrapped the large plush towel around his waist, and hurried to the front door, leaving foot tracks of water trailing behind him.

He opened the door, and immediately wished he'd asked who was it when he saw the person standing in front of him. He would have at least put on a robe to look more presentable. He hoped it might have been Cherise coming home to get some clothes, or something for work, but it wasn't. He was hoping to see her today, and if not this morning, he was prepared to go by her job with flowers. The same flowers he had picked up from the local grocery and brought home to an empty house last night.

He knew that he'd messed up with her a couple of nights ago. He didn't know what had come over him. He had never done anything like that before. He was planning to apologize to her for forcing himself on her the way he did, but when he came home last night, she wasn't there. He'd called her several times before she finally answered and told him that she was staying at her father's house for the night.

The lame excuse about needing some time didn't sit well with him, and he'd hoped she wasn't planning on leaving him. If she had been anywhere else, he would have gone to her. He wouldn't say that he was scared, but he wasn't in the mood to get into an altercation with his father-in-law about his daughter. He knew that Dellwood didn't care too much for him, and he didn't want to make a bad situation worse.

He didn't want to think the worse, but six-thirty was kind of early to be knocking on someone's door. That usually meant something was wrong. A lump formed in his throat as he prepared to greet his visitor.

"Yes. May I help you?"

"Are you Terrell Tillman?"

"Yes, I am."

"I have a restraining order for you, and it requires you to leave the premises immediately."

"A what?" Terrell was shocked by the news the officer just shared. "Are you kidding me?"

"No sir. I apologize, but you will need to hurry up and put some clothes on. You have to leave the premises."

Not talking to anyone in particular, but aggravated by the directive given by the officer, "Maaaaaan. You got to be … kidding… me," Terrell cried out with an elevated voice.

"Unfortunately sir, I do not have time to debate with you. It would be in your best interest to cooperate in this matter. I will give you a few minutes to get dressed, and time to gather a few things. If you do not comply, I will have to take you in for disorderly conduct."

"Do what?"

"Sir. I'm warning you."

Terrell lifted both his hands to signify he was surrendering and not wanting to cause any trouble. "Alright. Alright. I'll be done in a few minutes."

The officer didn't respond to Terrell anymore. He turned and walked away, and headed for his patrol car. He patiently waited as he gave Terrell the time and space needed to pack some of his belongings.

Moments later, Terrell came out of the house, with a duffle bag in tow. After a few trips back into the house, he locked and closed the door. When the officer saw that he was finished loading his truck, he greeted him with the copies of the paperwork.

"Mr. Tillman, you have been served. Have a nice day."

Terrell accepted the documents, and before he could muster up a response, the heartless officer had retreated back to his vehicle. Terrell studied the papers in his hands. He glanced over them, as he walked to his truck. *Divorce?... What the...?*

Since the officer only mentioned the restraining order, Terrell had no idea there were documents for a divorce. This caught him completely off guard.

The officer watched as Terrell threw a tantrum in the front yard, in response to the news he had just received. He started to get out of his patrol car and confront him, but decided against it when he noticed Terrell getting inside his truck. Although he was doing his job, he kind of felt sorry for the poor guy. What a way to start a day.

For a brief moment, Terrell sat quietly, trying to get himself together. The shock of the news had made him depressed and weak. When he felt that he was able to go on, he pulled out of the driveway, and against his own will, left the place he called home.

Chapter Twelve

Terrell sat at the foot of the bed in his hotel room. He didn't see this coming by a long shot. As much as he fought against it, he couldn't stop the tears from falling. Defeated, he rested his elbows, one on each knee, and leaned his face down into the palm of his hands. *Who does Cherise think she is—treating me like this? How could she do this? And she calls herself a Christian. Yeah, right.*

He laid back on the bed, with both hands behind his head for a pillow, and stared at the ceiling. Alone with his thoughts, he convinced himself that Cherise was messing around, and that she wanted to be with someone else. What else could it be? She never wanted to have sex, and when she did—she just lay there like a bump on a log.

His right side jerked from the vibration of his cell phone. He removed it from its holster, and screened the call. Besides waiting to hear from Cherise, this was the call he was also waiting for. He opened the phone, and placed it to his ear to answer the incoming call...

"Hello."

"Brother Tillman?" Pastor Revenew inquired. Terrell's voice was almost unrecognizable. The previously shed tears had drained into his nasal passage which made his voice distorted.

Clearing his throat, "Yes sir, this is me."

"I hardly recognized your voice. I got your message, and I called as soon as I could. Is everything okay?"

Helpless, he answered, "No! Everything is not okay. Cherise filed for a divorce."

Pastor Revenew bucked his eyes at the response. *A divorce?* He knew it had to be something serious for Terrell to call him. He seemed desperate in his message he left on the voicemail. Now talking to him—he felt sorry for him. He had never witnessed this meek side of Terrell before. He was usually defiant and argumentative. As a matter of fact, he was surprised that Terrell had called him in the first place, being that they never really saw eye to eye, and Terrell had made it clear, that he didn't need counsel from anyone but God Himself.

Terrell was one of those people that, after you've tried to help over and over again, and they refuse to listen, you just wanted to wash your hands of them. Nevertheless, as a pastor, he couldn't reject a man in need—even if it was Terrell. He had to be the bigger person, and lead by example.

"Did something happen? How do you know she filed for a divorce?"

"The police came to the house with a protective order and told me I had to leave, and that I couldn't come within so many feet of her. Then they served me with the divorce papers."

"I'm sorry to hear that, Brother Tillman. Have you talked to Cherise?"

"I've tried calling her several times, but she won't answer my calls. I thought maybe she had talked to you about it. Has she?"

"No. I haven't spoken to her for a few days." Until now, he hadn't realized that he hadn't spoken to Cherise since last Sunday—after service. He didn't attend this week's Bible study, due to a speaking engagement out of town. He'd been so busy that it hadn't dawn on him that she hadn't even called to give him a report on how Bible study went.

He couldn't help but to feel worried. *Something must have happened.* He didn't want to think the worst, but he knew that Cherise wouldn't have done something like this without a good reason. *A divorce and a restraining order? Hmm.*

"I had no idea that things had gotten this bad. Did anything happen to make her just jump up and file for a divorce?"

Terrell deceitfully answered, "No. Nothing happened. She didn't say anything to me at all—she just did it. I didn't even know she was thinking about a divorce."

"Hmm. Do you have any idea where she's at right now?"

"No. She won't answer my calls, or respond to my texts."

"Okay. Well I'm gonna try to call and talk to her. Are you going to be alright? Do you need anything?"

Terrell knew that if Cherise would talk to anybody, it would be Pastor Revenew. They had a special bond, and she highly respected his counsel.

"Just talk to her for me, please. Tell her to call me."

"I'll see what I can do."

"Thanks, Pastor Revenew. I appreciate it."

"No problem. I'll check on you later."

Pastor Revenew disconnected the call, and immediately called Cherise...

"Hello."

"Hey Sister Cherise, How's it going?"

"Hey Pastor. How are you?"

"I'm doing well. Is everything good with you?"

"Yep. Everything's fine."

He didn't want to be pushy, but it didn't seem like she was going to offer him the information he was seeking, so he just came straight out with it. "Brother Tillman called me today..."

Before he could finish his sentence, she interrupted, "He called you? He hasn't been calling you."

"That was the same thing I said, but he called me, to tell me, that you put him out of the house, and filed for a divorce. Is this true?"

"It is."

"May I ask why?"

"I'm tired pastor—I'm tired. I have tried to stay in this marriage as long as I could, and I'm just tired. And after he raped me the other night, I was done."

"Raped you?" he asked. "What do you mean raped you? That's your husband."

She told him the details of the incident, and his stomach turned with disgust. His initial thought was to call Terrell back, and tell him that he got what he deserved, but he knew that would not be the right thing to do. Instead, he had to do what God was leading him to do.

"I don't agree with his actions at all, and I'm definitely going to let him know this the next time I speak to him. What I want to know from you though is—are you sure you want to get a divorce? This is a very serious matter, and it is not something that should be done without deep consideration, and thought."

"Yeah, I know. I prayed, and I asked God for a sign, and I feel like he gave me one." She told him about her prayer, and how God answered.

"Well Sis. Cherise, just as God hears prayers, so does the devil."

"I know, but…"

"Let me ask you this—have you considered counseling?"

"I did, but when I asked Terrell about it once before, he told me that he didn't need any counseling. I just needed to learn to be obedient and submissive, and then everything would be fine."

Rolling his eyes, and shaking his head, "Yeah, that brother has a lot to learn."

"I'm just tired, Pastor. I'm tired of going to church praising God, and coming home fussing and fighting. I'm tired of him doing anything he feels like, and God allowing him to do it. I'm tired of him taking advantage of me. I'm tired of him using me, and I'm tired of crying. This can't be right. God can't possibly be pleased with this," she cried.

"He's not pleased, and I can certainly understand your frustration and pain. I'm so sorry you are going through this, but if he agrees to counseling, would you at least go?"

With a long moan, "I don't know. I'll have to think about it."

Not wanting to appear pushy, he digressed, "Fair enough. How are the girls?"

"They're good. We were just about to have dinner."

"Well, okay. Tell them both I said hi, and I'll talk to you later."

Chapter Thirteen

Cherise pulled into the driveway of the home of Dr. Ben Stanley. He was the counselor that she and Terrell had been seeing every Tuesday, at five o'clock in the evening, for the last three weeks. He was chosen because, Pastor Revenew actually interviewed him to make sure he was a Christian counselor, and that he believed the same things as they did. They all agreed that someone, who was ignorant to their situation, would be best for all parties involved.

Terrell was trying desperately to come back home, but Cherise was not willing to sacrifice so easily, her new "peace that passeth all understanding"— the name she gave the innovative serenity she now felt in her home, since Terrell had been gone. There was no arguing, no fighting, and best of all, no sex. She didn't miss that at all.

It wasn't that she disliked sex; she just didn't like doing it with Terrell. A mere stranger had better chances of satisfying her than he did. Terrell had done so many horrible things to her, that the constant abuse had produced an emotional detachment. Sex felt more like a chore, than a pleasurable, intimate experience. There was no passion, affection, love, or enjoyment. She felt more like a prostitute, but at least they got paid for it.

She thought that his absence would affect the kids, but even they seemed happier. They loved their daddy, but they were both mommy girls to the core. Just when she thought she was getting the bed to herself, she gained two midget roommates. Good thing there was no other man in her life.

Cherise was content, but a small piece of her felt sorry for Terrell—which is the only reason she agreed to postpone the divorce proceedings—until after they had tried counseling. They weren't making any progress, but Cherise was willing to attend a few more sessions—before just calling it quits.

She was sitting in the car, awaiting Terrell's arrival, so they could go into the meeting together, as they had done since day one. When she saw his car pull in behind hers, she checked the mirror to make sure no strands of hair was out of place. By the time she put on her lip gloss, Terrell was opening the door to assist her in getting out.

If she couldn't say anything else good about him, he was always a gentleman when it came to opening doors for a lady, except for when they were mad at each other—then she would open her own doors. They walked up to the solid Brazilian Mahogany door, and Cherise admired the unique glasswork that complemented the two sidelights. Terrell pressed the doorbell, and within seconds, Dr. Stanley opened the door, and greeted them as they walked inside. Oddly enough, his office was inside the home, up the stairs. He gestured for them to take the lead, and Terrell allowed Cherise to go first.

He remembered what Dr. Stanley had taught them on their first visit. Men should always allow ladies to walk in front of them, when going up stairs, but when coming down, the man should be first. This way—if she slips, or tumbles; the man would be in position to catch her, or at least prevent her fall. Neither Cherise, nor Terrell had heard this before, but when he explained it to them, it made perfect sense. Ever since then, whenever they came for their appointment, and approached the flight of steps, Cherise led the way up, and Terrell led the way down.

They had originally signed up for twelve sessions, and had managed to complete three of them. Last week's session proved—that if this marriage was going to be saved, they had a lot of work to do; starting with the basics. Dr. Stanley gave them a homework assignment that required them to write down what they felt their roles were as a husband and a wife. They were instructed not to discuss the assignment with each other, but rather to wait until this week's appointment to review.

Not long after they had entered the in-home office, and sat down, Dr. Stanley asked them to read their answers aloud. As customary, Cherise went first. Her responses were that of the norm—to support, to encourage, to be a helpmeet, to be submissive "as unto the Lord."

Terrell decided not to do the assignment because he felt that it was stupid, and he couldn't see the significance of it. After a brief explanation of why he gave the assignment, Dr. Stanley expressed to Terrell—that in order for counseling to be effective, he would need to at least be willing to participate. He explained that counseling only works when the people involved are serious, and genuinely wants to improve the situation.

That was the thing; Terrell didn't really want to go to counseling, he was just doing it, so that he could say he'd done it. He'd told Pastor Revenew that he would do anything if it meant he could come back home, and out of compassion for a man that seemed sincere in his efforts, the pastor convinced Cherise to go along with it.

Cherise had already made up in her mind that she wouldn't allow Terrell to come back home until—she felt he was making changes for the better. What she didn't want to happen was—as soon as he got what he wanted, she was afraid he would revert back to his old ways.

Dr. Stanley was messing up Terrell's plans with all his psychological evaluations and comments. He told Terrell that he was too arrogant, and very intimidating—and if he could make him feel that way as a man, then he could only imagine how he was making Cherise feel. Of course, this made him angry, and he became confrontational with both, the therapist and Cherise.

After going back and forth, for about thirty minutes, Dr. Stanley abruptly bellowed, "ENOUGH". The tone he had taken startled both Terrell and Cherise. He removed his specs, and sat them on a stack of papers, sitting on his desk. He closed his eyes, as he massaged his temples, and an uncomfortable, chilling silence rested in the room.

Dr. Stanley had become awkwardly taciturn for what seemed like forever. When he finally spoke, the words that came from his lips left them in shock. He calmly told them that he could no longer assist them. In a four week period, they had not made any progress, and he could definitely see why their relationship was in a dying state. He was surprised that Cherise lasted as long as she had, without needing professional therapy herself. On the other hand, Terrell was a hot mess, and he needed to be admitted into a psych ward for serious evaluation.

He thought it was very commendable of Pastor Revenew to take an interest in saving their marriage, but there was nothing more he could do. At a certain point, a person has to want help, and it appeared that Terrell didn't want any, and Cherise was not backing down. He was too stubborn, and arrogant, and she was so fed up, that she had developed a hard heart in the process. She had also become stubborn, but in a good way. She was finally standing up for herself, and was not subjecting herself to anymore abuse—of any kind. Who could really blame the poor girl?

*****

On her way home, Cherise called Sasha and Sybill on three-way, to tell them what had just transpired…

"Are you both there?" Cherise asked.

Imitating kids in class, answering at roll call "Heeere," Sasha sang.

"I'm here," Sybill answered. "What done happened now?"

"Why you think something happened?" Cherise asked, while laughing at Sybill's tone.

Sasha remained quiet, but Sybill responded to the question. "Oh, something happened—so you might as well quit playing and gon' and tell us.

"OK—OK. Are y'all ready for this?"

Simultaneously, they chimed, "Whaaat?"

"The counselor kicked us out."

"You lying," Sasha announced with unbelief.

"Quit playing," Sybill insisted.

"I'm not. He basically told us there was no help for us, and he refused to work with us any longer."

Sympathetically, "Wow, Cherise! I am sooooo sorry to hear that," Sasha said. "Are you alright?"

"Yeah, I"m fine. It is what it is."

"That's a darn shame. You know it's bad when the counselor throws you out. Girrrrl, that car got too many miles on it, and it's not even worth fixing. So—when it gets to this point—you can either sell it, give it away, or trade it in for a new one. Either way, you don't need to keep it around because, it will cost you too much in the end."

They all laughed at Sybill's life lesson. She always had a funny analogy for a situation. Nevertheless, she got her messages across and a good laugh in at the same time.

"Sybill you need to quit your mess," Sasha said, while laughing at the same time.

"Girl, I ain't playing. She needs to get rid of that fool."

Cherise could always count on her friends to make her feel better, and she could always count on Sybill to add some comedy in her drama-filled life.

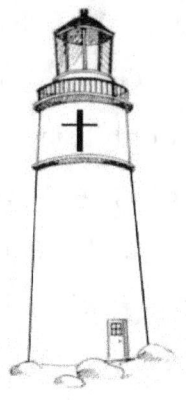

Chapter Fourteen

Three months had passed, and Terrell finally decided to move into his own place. Shortly after, he accepted another opportunity to serve active duty, to work as security on Fort Stewart. This opportunity couldn't have come at a better time because he needed the extra money to help pay for all of his new expenses.

When he first left, he called Cherise every, single, day. Then all of a sudden, the calls decreased from every single day—to every other day—to once a week—to once every two weeks. It was obvious, based on his actions, something or somebody was occupying his time. Cherise was actually quite happy about him not calling as much, but what bothered her was—when he did call, he only requested to speak to Alysa. He totally disregarded Alyson and her feelings. He did, however, reply to her message and sent her an email that would leave an everlasting knife in her heart...

Hey Ally Pooh,

I'm so glad to hear from you. I'm doing pretty good, I just miss seeing you guys and of course, being able to sleep in my own bed. Good thing I am only a few hours away from home. I am very happy to know that you made all A's and B's on your recent report card. I am so proud of you! Keep up the good work!

I'm sure you know by now that me and your mom are planning on getting a divorce and once we do, I won't be able to be your daddy anymore. It's not what I wanted but it's what your mom wanted, so I will just have to deal with it, I guess.

I'm sure that your mom will meet someone new, if she hasn't already, and when she does, it will be his job to be your daddy, and I don't want to be in the way. I can only hope that you will treat him with the same respect as you did me, and if he is any kind of man, he will take care of you like I did. Please don't take this personal, because it's not. I still love you as I have always loved you, and I always will. If you need anything, please don't hesitate to call me. If I can help you, I will. In the meantime, continue to do good in school, and be a good girl and help your mom with your sister.

Love,

Terrell

Oh my God... Cherise stared at the computer screen in disbelief. Angry tears flooded her face, as she held her weeping child in her arms. She knew that Terrell was low down, but even he couldn't possibly be so heartless—to hurt an innocent child.

Sure his name wasn't on the birth certificate, but he was the only daddy Alyson really knew. She was only two years old when Terrell and Cherise started dating, and she fell in love with him right away. Besides him being a good lover, Alyson's loving attachment to Terrell is what added the icing on the cake, when it came to Cherise making the decision to be his girlfriend.

Little Alyson was so fond of him that she'd created her own little song and dance to announce his arrival, whenever she heard the distinguished sounds of the white Z-24 pull in the driveway. "Terrell Terrell" she would sing—over and over again, until he walked through the door and picked her up and flew her around like an airplane. From that time, until now—that was her daddy, and he had just ripped out her little heart.

His letter couldn't have come at a worse time, because Dellwood was walking through the door, demanding to know what was wrong with his granddaughter. For some reason, he didn't feel he needed to knock, or needed permission to enter his own daughter's house.

When Cherise explained to him what happened, he was furious. Dellwood was nowhere near being saved, so his mouth could be atrocious.

"That boy is going to make me kill him about my children. How you gon' be in somebody's life all them years, and then tell them you can't be their daddy no mo'? He must don't know who he's messing with. He can't."

This was what Cherise feared, because once Dellwood got upset, there was no calming him down. All she could do was sit quietly and let him finish fussing…

"That boy can't say nothing else to me as long as he lives. He done messed up with me! If I was driving down the road, and saw him standing on fire, and all I had to do was spit on him to save his life…he is as good as dead. Ashes to ashes, dust to dust. I promise to God he would because, (shaking his head from side to side) you just don't do children like that— especially one of mine."

With each round, his voice rose higher and higher. "You shouldn't have told me this. This right here done got my blood pressure up." Now pointing his finger toward the floor to put emphasis on what he was saying…

"I'm telling you right now, Cherise, I don't want him back in this house. If I ever catch him over here, I'ma shove my boot so far down his throat… I am not lying… I am gonna kill that boy, and then I'ma get you for letting him in here. You hear me?" he yelled. Without waiting for a response, he stormed out of the house, and slammed the door.

Cherise was hurt because, there was absolutely nothing she could do. The fact remained, that Alyson was not Terrell's biological child, and the law prevailed in this matter.

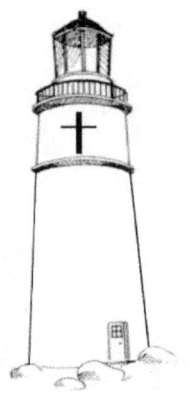

Chapter Fifteen

Lately, Cherise had been feeling some kind of way. Her emotions and thoughts were all over the place. Frustrated, mainly because she couldn't quite articulate to anyone exactly what she was feeling. No words could explain what s e was going through.

She knew that God was calling her higher, and had been for a while. The only problem was—she didn't know what He was calling her to. She knew that He was requiring something mighty of her, but what?

She had recently attended a women's prayer breakfast function that Sasha had invited her and Sybill to. Sasha was excited because she was asked to give an inspirational word, and she wanted her friends to be there to support her. Cherise almost changed her mind about going, but she didn't want to let her friend down, and she knew she would enjoy herself once there.

She loved worshipping with other women because the fellowship was different than that of a regular church service with both ladies and men. Women were not afraid to release themselves, and be free. Women were not afraid to share their failures, faults, mistakes, and experiences, so that other women could learn from them, and be edified. Women were not ashamed to strip them-selves before others, so that they could get what they needed from the Lord. The worship experience with women was always refreshing, refueling, and reviving.

Many women ministered that day, but the message delivered by the First Lady of the house, ministered to Cherise the most. She talked about the importance of putting God first, and the benefits of it. She taught on how the Lord instructs, guides and directs the footsteps of those that seek Him.

She talked about the daily deposits of wisdom that are gained through spending time with the Lord, and how He prepares the heart to deal with issues that may arise from day-to-day. She demonstrated how God's wisdom teaches balance and creative ways of doing all the things that's required of the many roles of a woman. Her tone demanded the attention from everyone under the sound of her voice. Her words captivated her audience, and her passion for God was beautifully expressed as she shared her testimony.

Sasha's First Lady was a magnificent speaker, and her teachings motivated Cherise to start a new daily regimen. Although New Year's was only a few weeks away, she decided to start on her resolution early. For the last two weeks, Cherise had faithfully awakened every morning at five o'clock to pray and read her Bible. The first couple of days were a struggle, but it became easier with each passing day. Full of determination, she began to seek God with zeal, like never before.

This morning, as she prayed silently with her eyes closed, in the quiet, dark filled room, she became frozen at the sight before her. In a flash, she saw herself carrying people out of a burning building. Unbelievably, she was reliving the same dream she had dreamt almost two years ago, but this time was different. This time she was definitely not asleep—she was alert, attentive, and wide awake.

As soon as the vision faded, she heard a still small voice loud and clear... "Yes, you were called to save many lives, but before you can save anyone else's life, you must first save your own husband out of the fire."

Unrestricted tears streamed down her face, as an electrifying emotion arose within her. With trembling and fear, she stood and lifted her hands in complete surrender to the spiritual arrest. "Yes Lord. Yes Lord," she repeated countless times, as she cried aloud. Minutes later, her praise became filled with melodies of an unknown tongue. She was no longer in control, but under submission to the Holy Spirit.

Full of awe, Cherise embraced the personal encounter she'd just experienced with God. She'd received many prophecies—people saying, "God said this" and "God said that", but never had she heard His voice before, herself. As amazing as this experience was, she was a little disturbed.

When she needed the meaning of the dream, He didn't answer. After months of absolutely no answers or help, she gave up on her search, and tossed it away from her psyche. *So why now, after all this time?*

Her mind ran through a list of questions—*What just happened? What did I just agree to do? Why are you calling him my husband? Save Terrell from what? Save him how?*

"First Peter, three and one," a soft voice spoke.

"First Peter, three and one?" she questioned, as she repeated what she heard with a whisper. She thought she might have been talking to herself, but she knew that wasn't a scripture she had memorized for herself. She picked up her Full Life Study Bible, and flipped through the pages until she found the scripture that was in her head.

"Likewise, ye wives, be in subjection to your own husbands; that, if any obey not the word, they also may without the word be won by the conversation of the wives." *What does this mean?* She read the text again. She could have understood it, if she and Terrell were still together. They were nearly divorced. *Ok, Lord... What does this mean? Me and Terrell are not together, and I do not want to win him.*

As much as she tried to put that scripture out of her mind, everywhere she turned; there it was—popping up in the strangest places. Every time she would open her Bible, no matter what she was looking for, it would automatically land on the same page. One time she tried to open the Bible in the middle, and it slipped and fell on the floor. When she picked it up, there it was again.

"Likewise, ye wives, be in subjection to your own husbands; that, if any obey not the word, they also may without the word be won by the conversation of the wives."

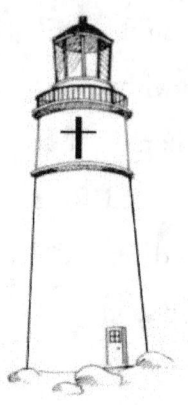

Chapter Sixteen

Two-thousand and three was an extremely long year, and Cherise was glad it was over. Through all the heartaches, struggles, and tears—she made it. She had to crawl sometimes, but she made it. There were times she had a limp, but she made it. She even had to be carried sometimes, but thankfully—she made it.

Today was the first Sunday in two-thousand and four, and she was ready to give God all the praises that were due to Him. She had so much to be thankful for. He had kept her in more ways than one, but most of all, he kept her from losing her mind during all she endured the last year. So, with uplifted hands, and a grateful heart, she stood behind the mic, and began to lead the congregation into worship.

She'd hoped they were ready because she was on a spiritual high. The praise she had on the inside of her belly could no longer be contained. Either they would get onboard, or get left behind, but she was going to praise God, even if she had to do it all by herself.

Apparently, the majority of the people must have come with the same mindset. The worship was nothing less than spectacular, and she was pleased with the response she was getting from the audience. As the praise team ministered their final selection, Pastor Revenew stood from his seat on the pulpit, and lifted his hands in the air. Indescribable waves and waves of God's presence swept the entire sanctuary and all the people, in their own individual way—praised God. Some wept, some wailed, some lifted their hands, some flooded the altar, some shouted, and some even passed out.

It was now time for the Word to go forth, but Pastor Revenew was careful not to interfere with what God was doing. After he saw that the Spirit had lifted enough to proceed with the Word—he greeted the congregation, read his selected scriptures, and delivered an anointed sermon on forgiveness. As the musicians softly played—"Breathe" by the

Christian worship leader, Michael W. Smith, Pastor Revenew told a story to add more meaning to his message…

"Many years ago, my Bishop's wife left him without a word. She had affairs with different men, and conceived a child—not once, not twice, but on three different occasions. Every time she would come back home, he would take her back, along with her children. For the life of me, I couldn't understand how he could keep taking her back after doing the same thing over and over again." Turning his head from side to side, "I don't think—No—I know I couldn't have done it."

"When I had a chance to be alone with him, I asked him about it, because I wanted to know how he could stay with her after the infidelity. With a soft and convicting tone, he said to me, "Isn't that what the cross, Jesus' death and resurrection is all about? Forgiveness? If not—what is it all about then? What are we preaching about then? How can we preach it, and declare it, but not do it?

"When I left him, I had a new outlook on what it means to be called by God, and the meaning of forgiveness. Today, God wants to give you a new level and understanding of what forgiveness really is. Not only are some of you needing forgiveness from God, but some of you need to forgive others who have offended you. The altar is open to you to come and allow God to touch your hearts and do only what He can do."

People young and old flooded the altar in tears, looking for a special touch from the Lord. Pastor Revenew continued, "Some of you today are in the place where someone has hurt you and you're having a hard time forgiving them because you don't feel that they are worthy of forgiveness, but the Bible teaches us that God can't forgive us, if we don't forgive others. Furthermore, forgiveness is more about you than it is the other person.

"Forgiveness is like a self-healing agent. It starts a process internally that helps us to heal and move on with life. Forgiveness helps prevent the seeds that Satan tries to plant in our hearts from taking root—seeds such as bitterness, resentment, and anger. As we hold on to the belief that someone has done something to us so bad that we cannot, will not, forgive—we give power to that part of us that feels vulnerable.

"I know that you feel like if you forgive that person, you are letting them off the hook, or so-called giving in, but holding onto grudges, or the hurt only keeps you bound. I will not lie, sometimes it still hurts, but when you really forgive, it doesn't hurt as bad. It doesn't even mean you won't remember, but it won't hinder you from moving forward in life and in God. I'm begging you to come, and release them, and all your hurts to Him." Pointing to the ceiling, "There is no hurt that God can not heal."

More people walked into the aisle, and to the altar seeking solace for their pain. It was evident that this was a Rhema Word, sent straight from heaven. Pastor Revenew was in tears as he continued his bidding...

"Some of you in here today, said with your lips, that you forgave that person that hurt you, but you know deep down that you haven't—you need to come today. Let not another day go by and you are still holding on to this thing any longer. It's time to let it go, and let it go for real. Saying "I forgive you" is more than lip service, but it starts in the heart. You might can't do it on your own, but God is here to help you. Let Him help you."

Cherise battled with the thought of going to the altar. Her heart was telling her one thing, but her mind was saying something else. She sat in her seat as long as she could, but when First Lady Revenew came and extended her hand to her, she knew she couldn't stay put any longer.

First Lady Anita Revenew was a very elegant lady—truly meek, humble, and beautiful inside and out. She was also very stylish, always sporting the hottest suits, with matching hats and pumps. By looking at her, you wouldn't know it, but she had a special healing anointing. It wasn't often, but it always manifested when the services were high like today, and when the Spirit led her to move, she moved.

With tear-filled eyes, Cherise grabbed her hand, stood, and received the hug that Mother Revenew was offering. She rested in her loving embrace, and cried like a baby. As First Lady Revenew began to pray, the Spirit rested upon Cherise, and ministered to her soul. Moments later, she fell to the floor, as the Spirit became too much for her to handle. One of the ushers came to her aid, and covered her with a white sheet.

When Cherise came to, the service was almost over. Pastor Revenew was giving his final remarks, and getting ready to do the benediction. The altar call lasted for nearly an hour, but when it was over; many people were blessed, healed, and delivered. Truly, the presence of the Lord was in New Harvest Christian Ministries, and as for Cherise, she would never be the same again.

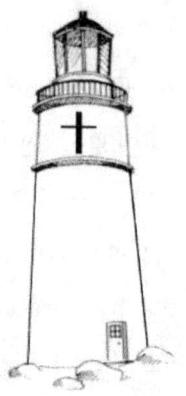

Chapter Seventeen

While driving home from church, Cherise decided to call Terrell, but he didn't answer. She left a message, telling him that she needed to talk to him—whenever he had time. She knew what she had to do. She had heard from God, and was now ready to forgive Terrell.

It's funny how things change. She laughed at the thought of her response to some of the church members a few months back. Each conversation was identical to the other.

"Hey Sis. Tillman. How are you?"

"I'm fine, and you?"

"Good. I heard about you and Bro. Tillman, and I just wanted to let you know that I was praying for you guys and your marriage."

"Noooooooooo! Don't pray for our marriage, just pray that God's will be done."

As silly as it may have sounded, Cherise was serious about not wanting people to pray because—she knew just how powerful prayer really was, and she had no intentions of being reconciled with Terrell. However, God had been dealing with her since right before the holidays, and she'd told Him that she would reconcile with her husband if—that was what He wanted her to do. So, there it was today—God had confirmed what He had been whispering in her spirit.

Later that evening, she decided to take the girls to see a movie. Terrell had returned her call, and told her that he was in town for the day, but would be leaving early in the morning to go back to Fort Stewart. She offered to let him come with them to the movies, but he declined the offer, in order to pack up everything he needed to take back with him.

When they returned home, Terrell was sitting in the driveway waiting. Alysa was screaming "daddy" to the top of her lungs, and could hardly wait to get out of the car. Alyson on the other hand, was quiet, and didn't show any excitement at his arrival. When Cherise unlocked the door to the house, Alyson went straight to her room, and shut the door. She didn't want anything to do with Terrell, and he knew it.

His heart ached because, he truly did love her, but he had allowed his own personal issues and feelings to get the best of him. Now, his actions had hurt his Ally Pooh, and he couldn't have felt any lower than he felt at that moment. He asked Cherise if it was alright for him to go and talk to her—she agreed. He went to the closed door and knocked on it, and seconds later he entered the room.

While Terrell and Alyson talked, Cherise gave Alysa a bath, and prepared her for bed. Shortly after, Terrell came out of Alyson's room, and found Cherise and Alysa sitting on the sofa in the living room, watching *That's So Raven*.

"Is that all y'all ever watch? That's what that chap in there is watching too," he said, referring to Alyson.

"Pretty much. It's what they like."

"Yeah, right. I think the mama likes it just as much as the kids," he said jokingly.

Cherise couldn't help but laugh, because she knew his statement was true. "You're right." She just got a kick out of all the ridiculous, hilarious situations the stylish teen got herself, her family and friends into from her undeveloped abilities to see into the future. For a kids' show, it was comedy at its best.

Shifting the direction of the conversation, Terrell asked, "So, what did you want to talk to me about?"

"Hold on for a moment," she instructed. She told Alysa to go in the room with Alyson so that she could talk to daddy for a minute, and she did as she was told. When Cherise felt that it was safe to speak, she removed all her layers of hurt and pride, and bared her heart. She told him that she'd forgiven him for all the things he had ever done to her, and that she was willing to give their marriage another try if he wanted to.

Terrell was dumbfounded. Just as it was with the restraining order and divorce, he didn't see this coming either. He was speechless. Had she proposed this to him three months ago, he would had dropped everything and come running back—however, he was now serving a full year on active duty, and he had just signed a year's lease on an apartment. This is what he had been begging for—for nearly six months, and just when he had conditioned himself to move on without her, she changes her mind.

Cherise assured him that he didn't have to feel pressured, and if he didn't want to come back home, she would understand, and they could still be friends. She knew a lot of time had passed, and if he had started dating someone else, she would completely understand. Either way, she didn't hate him anymore, and wanted to let him know that she had forgiven him for everything he'd ever done to her.

They talked for about another thirty minutes, and the conversation ended on a good note. They decided to take things slow, and agreed to only date each other while he was serving his tenure. After that, they would decide what happened next.

After she and Terrell finished their conversation, he asked if he could use the computer to check his email. She told him while he was doing that, she needed to run to the store for a few things. She asked if he wasn't in a hurry, could he stay with the girls until she returned.

While she was on her way to the store, she remembered that she'd left something she needed to return. She did a circle around the block, and parked on the side of the road, in front of the mailbox. Terrell didn't hear her come back, so when she opened the door, she startled him. When he realized who it was, he quickly closed his cell phone, hanging up on the person on the other end.

Cherise was standing next to him when the caller called back. She could hear the woman on the other end ask, "What happened? Did you hang up?" She could see that Terrell was nervous, but pretended not to notice. She went to her room and got the item she planned to return, and when she came back to the living room, he had ended the call.

"Who was that?" she curiously asked.

"Oh, that was my homeboy Tony."

"Well Tony sure sounded like a woman to me."

"That wasn't no woman. I told you... that was my homeboy from back at Fort Stewart. He was just calling to see if I was coming back tonight, so we could go hang out."

"No problem," Cherise said, grabbing for his phone. "If that was your homeboy, you won't mind calling him back." Sarcastically, she queried, "There was no need to hang up in his face—if that was your homeboy. There was no need to rush him off the phone—if that was your homeboy. So, let's just call your homeboy back," she said, while holding up quotation marks every time she said the word, "homeboy".

He stood up from the computer chair, and put the phone in his jacket pocket. "Cherise stop. I'm not calling him back, and make myself look like a fool for you. I'll be the laughing stock on base."

"Umm Hmm. Whatever Terrell." Cherise walked out the house, and left him standing in the middle of the floor. One thing she was not—was a fool. So if he thought she believed them lies, he had another think coming—and since he had to lie, she would find out whom it was on her own.

When she returned home from the store, Terrell was asleep across her bed. She knew that he would be leaving sometime in the wee hours of the morning, so she allowed him to sleep. And just so she didn't forget about the phone call from the "homeboy" named Tony, she pulled out a notepad, and wrote—January 4, 2004, and right underneath it, she wrote—8:21 p.m.

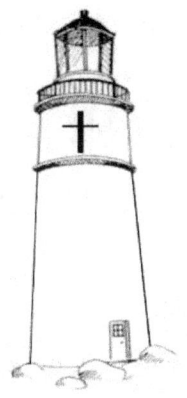

Chapter Eighteen

The drive back to Fort Stewart was not too bad. The nap Terrell took, along with the early morning sex he'd just had with Cherise, and a hot shower, was all he needed to get him ready for his three-hour commute. After his arrival, he called Cherise as promised to let her know that he'd made it safely to his destination.

Cherise was already up, reading one of her many devotionals that she received daily in her email, from one of the many ministries she'd signed up for. This morning while on the computer, she logged onto Cingular Wireless' website, and tried to register Terrell's cell phone number. Her plan was to register the account and set it up for detailed billing. Once the new bill printed, she would find the number that called his phone on the noted date and time.

Unfortunately, she was unable to set up the account online without having the actual account number. *Shoot, shoot, shoot… darn it! Oh well, no problem. I'll just call Cingular after they open, and get the information.* By the time she got to work, and got settled at her desk, she figured this would be a good time to call, and get the information she needed to set up the account.

As she dialed the customer service number for the cellular company, she smiled at the fact that she was way smarter than Terrell thought she was. She was a lot of things, but dumb wasn't one of them. Actually, she was too smart for her own good—as she would soon find out.

"Thank you for choosing Cingular Wireless, my name is Susan. How may I help you?"

"Yes, good morning, Susan. I'm trying to set up our account online in order to view the bill and start making payments via the internet, but I need our actual account number to do so."

"I'll be more than happy to help you with that. May I have the number you are calling about please?

Cherise gave the friendly lady the number, and verified all the information needed in order for the representative to access the records. As one customer service professional to another, Cherise knew exactly how to communicate with the woman, and found favor with the representative.

"Thank you. Ok, it shows that you have a family plan, with two phones that share 900 minutes per month. Is that correct?"

Cherise mouthed dropped. *A family plan?* Last she'd known, they didn't have a family plan. Terrell had his own individual plan, and she had hers. She didn't ask for all this. All she wanted was the account number. She had no idea she was biting off more than she could chew, but she wouldn't let on to the representative that she didn't know about the new line. She felt an uneasiness in the pit of her belly, as she prepared herself for the information she was about to receive. "Uh, yes….that is correct. The second phone is for a friend of ours. I can never remember that number, so can you give it to me please?"

Just like that, the representative gave her the number. "I'll be more than happy to. Let me know when you're ready to write it down."

Nervously, she said, "I'm ready." Cherise wrote down the number and felt a wave of anxiousness come over her when she realized the telephone number's area code was from the Savannah area—close to Fort Stewart. "Thank you so much."

"No problem. If you're ready, the account number is…"

"Uh…Oh, yes." Cherise had forgotten all about the account number, which was the reason she called in the first place. Her new found information had taken her aback, and all she wanted to do was get off the phone. "Thank you again."

"You're welcome, Mrs. Tillman. Is there anything else I can do for you?"

"No, you've done enough… literally."

"Okay—if there's nothing else, it's been my pleasure to assist you this morning and it was my goal to provide you with excellent customer service. Have I done that for you, Mrs. Tillman?"

"Yes you have."

"Great. Thank you for choosing Cingular Wireless. Have a great day."

Cherise looked at the number she had written down, and contemplated whether she should call it or not. One part of her wanted to know who the number belonged to, and another part of her, was scared to find out. When she couldn't make a sound decision, she sought advice from her girls, Sasha and Sybill.

Cherise sent both ladies an email, advising them that she really needed to talk to them at lunch. They decided to ride with her to the nearby Wendy's to grab something quickly, so they could sit in the car to discuss whatever issues Cherise was dealing with.

"Cherise, I think you need to pray on it before calling that number," Sasha said, concernedly.

"Bump that. Call now and pray later," Sybill objected. "Sasha knows good and well she would call that number so, I don't even know why she is sitting up there trying to act like she wouldn't," she said, angrily.

"I didn't say I wouldn't call, Sybill. I'm only suggesting that she pray first. She needs to allow God to lead and guide her in how to approach the situation."

"Oh—so you telling me—that if you found out your husband was cheating or that he had bought another woman a phone, you would take time to pray first?"

"Yes!" Sasha defended herself.

"Alright you guys. Enough," Cherise interrupted. "I need you two to stay sane, so you can help me through this."

"I'm sorry, Cherise. You're right," Sasha said, apologetically. "I still say you need to pray first. Again, I am not saying I wouldn't call, because I'm pretty sure I would.

BUT…." Looking at Sybill, and then, back at Cherise. "You need to be in the right frame of mind when you call that number. You need to ask God to prepare you for whatever you might find out."

"I guess you're right, Sasha," Cherise agreed.

"Boy, I tell you. This sandwich is just too messy to eat. The mayo is too slippery, the bologna is old, the bread is molded, and we ain't gon' even now talk about the cheese," Sybill said with a disgusted frown on her face, and her lips tooted up.

Cherise and Sasha looked at each other, and fell out laughing. They knew Sybill wasn't talking about her lunch from Wendy's because, she ordered nuggets today. Sasha was nearly in tears. "Where on earth do you come up with this stuff, girl?"

"Girl, I don't know. It just comes up, so I say it. Either way—this situation is a hot mess!"

This is something they could all agree on. This was definitely, a messy situation. Their lunch break was over, and they had to return to their individual departments. The ladies departed the vehicle, and laughed all the way back in the building at Sybill's animated analogies.

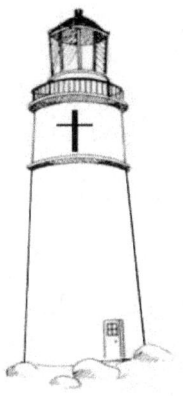

Chapter Nineteen

Four o'clock couldn't get here fast enough. Cherise was eager to get off of work and get home. She prayed, just as Sasha suggested, all the way home. She really didn't know what to expect, so she prepared herself to be ready for anything. She stopped and picked up an eight piece of chicken for dinner, and once she had fed the girls, she retreated to her room for privacy.

She pulled out the piece of paper she had written the number on, and briefly stared at it. She retrieved her cell phone from her pocket, and entered the star symbol, followed by the numbers, six and seven, before entering the telephone number Susan had given her. This would keep her number from showing on the other person's caller ID. Once she had pressed the call button, she held the phone to her ear, and closed her eyes as she listened to the rings on the other end.

"Hello." A soft feminine voice answered.

Cherise quickly hung up the phone. She wasn't as prepared as she thought she was. She quickly rehearsed her lines, of the script she had created for herself, to say to the other woman. She closed her eyes, counted to ten, took a deep breath, and redialed the number again—being sure to block her number as before.

"Hello." The same voice answered.

"Hi. I'm sorry to bother you, but my name is Cherise, and I'm Terrell's wife."

"Excuse me? Did you say wife?" the woman asked, confused.

"Yes—I'm his wife. The reason I called you is because I found this number attached to his cell account, and I wanted to know who the number belonged to. Didn't he tell you he was married?"

"No—he didn't. Actually, he told me that he was divorced."

"Separated, yes; but divorced—I don't think so. If you don't mind, may I ask your name?"

"Sure. My name is Tonisha, but they call me Toni for short."

"So, you're the homeboy, Tony that called him back last night?"

"Homeboy?" the lady inquired.

"Yes. Last night when you called—I asked him who it was, and he said you were his homeboy, Tony. How long have you and Terrell been talking?"

"I met Terrell a little over two months ago. I had been having problems with my phone, so he offered to buy me one, and add me to his plan. I didn't want to, but he gave it to me as a Christmas present."

Cherise found herself getting a little agitated. "Have y'all slept together?"

"Um.....Yeah," Toni answered. "But had I known he was married, I would have never talked to him. I'm saved, and I would never mess with a married man."

Cherise found it interesting that Toni felt compelled to tell her that she was saved—And the fact that she was sleeping with a man period, no matter if he was married or not, was sin. "It's still sin!" Cherise outbursted, before she knew it.

"I know, but it wouldn't be as bad, if he wasn't some-one else's husband." Toni didn't like the tone Cherise had taken with her and wanted to set her straight. "I didn't say I was perfect... I said I was saved, and I know that sleeping with a man, without being married is wrong."

"I'm sorry. I didn't mean to be judgmental. I'm just a little upset because—I just asked Terrell last night..."

"Last night?" Toni interrupted. "He was with you last night?"

"Yes. Last night. I just asked him last night, if he was messing with someone, and he lied and said no. Had he said yes, then I would have accepted the fact that he was, because I was the one who put him out. Instead, he lied." Cherise thought about something she'd once heard T.D. Jakes say in one of his sermons. *"Some people, when they get up in the morning, have to have a cup of coffee, and some people just have to have a lie."*

"He lied to me too—and I know when I ask him about you, he's going to lie and say it's not true."

"Of course he is."

"Well you don't have to worry about it anymore, because after today, it's over."

As much as Cherise wanted to believe Toni, she knew deep down that it wouldn't end just like that. Not with Terrell wining and dining her like she knew he was. She knew first hand, how sweet he could be in the beginning. Toni was saved, but she was a woman first. Although it seemed like a lifetime ago, Cherise was in this same place at one time. Remembering her own experience when she found out about Terrell's first wife, she knew that it wasn't easy to turn feelings on and off just like that. Who knows…maybe she's stronger than I was, but I doubt it.

Cherise cringed at the thought of Terrell and Toni having sex, and a hint of jealousy arose in her heart. In a matter of minutes, she became angry as she recalled her conversation with Terrell. She had just told him that she'd forgiven him for everything. If she didn't know any better, it was like the devil himself was listening at their conversation and said, "oh yeah…. you can forgive the past, but let's see if you can forgive this."

It was as if he had orchestrated the perfect plan of destruction, and Cherise was his target. He had patiently waited for the perfect moment, and it had finally arrived. At his signal, his plan would be set in motion, and all hell would break loose. With only a morsel of strength remaining, she apologized to her husband's lover, and thanked her for taking her call.

There was really nothing else to say, so she just hung up the phone. She felt betrayed by both, Terrell and God. Terrell's betrayal didn't hurt as bad as God's betrayal. He was the cause of all of this, and He made her care, when she didn't care at all. God knew all things, and that means, he knew this, but He still allowed her to set herself up for heartbreak. She didn't know which would have been worse—disobeying God, or being betrayed by God.

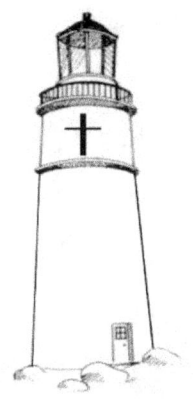

Chapter Twenty

"Don't go...don't leave...stay here...hold me...I know...and you know...tonight is the night...baby." Terrell sang and bobbed his head to the compelling sultry sounds of Jerzee Monet. He was introduced to her music by one of the guys on post, and found her style to be different than any music he had ever heard.

Whenever riding, he played music according to his mood, and today was a lovely kind of day. All was well in Terrell's world, and he was ready for an enjoyable night with Toni. He looked in the rearview mirror, for the umpteenth time and smiled. *Umph, I look good!* He resembled a delectable pot of gumbo, compiled of all good ingredients—he looked good and smelled good. If I'm lucky, before the night is over, I will feel good too.

He giggled at the thought he'd just had about feeling good, and decided to phone Toni to let her know he was on his way. It had been three days since he'd last seen her, and he could tell by how many times she'd called him while he was away, that she missed him. A part of him missed her too.

Tonisha Smalls, better known as Toni, was the complete opposite of Cherise. She was tall and slender, dark-skinned with a short haircut. She was very fit, and worked out at the local fitness center at least four times a week, which is where she and Terrell met. It never failed, whenever she was there, he would soon be coming through the double glass doors.

They had become well acquainted during his visits, and soon began dating, only after a few weeks. Love was in the air, and their relationship was blossoming rather quickly. With Toni occupying his time, Terrell had no need to bother Cherise anymore.

Toni didn't answer the first time Terrell called, so he waited a few minutes and tried calling her again—but still no answer. He thought it was strange, but didn't think too much of it. He figured she was probably in the shower, or getting dressed. He'd just see her when he got there.

He'd planned the perfect evening. They would go to downtown Savannah and enjoy a nice dinner at Ruth's Chris Steak House, and then a movie afterwards. He knew that their dinner would be a bit pricey, but he didn't mind at all. He was extremely happy, and felt like he had just hit the jackpot. Now that Cherise was back in the picture, he had the best of both worlds—a lady here and one back home.

He began putting together his game plan, while riding back to the base this morning. He would call Cherise every day while he was away, and spend as much time with Toni as he possibly could while there. On his off days, he would go home, and spend time with Cherise.

Toni would never suspect a thing. She was used to him going back home on his off days anyway. She understood that he needed to check on his apartment, check his mail, pay bills and things like that. All he had to do was call her, like he would do Cherise, when he was away.

He'd never done anything like this before, but he could see how a man could get used to it. Of course, he would need to come up with a budget plan, because having two women could get expensive. Double the birthdays, holidays, anniversaries, and not to mention the just because days. He was big on "just because" days because he loved the response he received due to the unexpected surprises—usually sex.

His unfinished planning session was put on pause, as he arrived at Toni's house. He horsed the motor a few times, turned off the engine, and exited the truck. As he approached the door, he pressed the doorbell, and waited for Toni to let him in. She opened the door, he smiled, but she didn't smile back. He tried to kiss her, but she pulled away.

He could tell something was wrong because ordinarily, she would jump right in his arms and greet him with a beautiful smile, passionate kiss and a warm embrace. She would normally be all over him.

He also noticed she wasn't dressed for going out. Maybe she's sick. Before he could ask her what was wrong, she went in on him, and dumped everything that she knew, out on the table.

As Toni was speaking, better yet, yelling, Terrell eyes bucked as wide as they could. He tried to respond but the words were trapped behind the lump that had formed in his throat. He could hear her talking, but she no longer had his full attention. He was more focused on trying to figure out how Cherise could have possibly found out about Toni.

After recovering from the initial shock that his secret was out, he tried to convince Toni that he and Cherise were over. He admitted to lying about being married, and explained his reason for doing so was only because he didn't want her to pre-judge him before getting to know him first. He didn't think that she would understand, and the truth would only complicate things.

Why should he miss out on a promising relationship with some-one, just because of some legalities? As far as he was concerned, when he put down the deposit on his own apartment, he was divorced. He had finally accepted the fact that he and Cherise were over, and made up his mind to move on with his life.

When he met Toni, he was indeed a single man. Cherise had made it perfectly clear, that she had no intentions on taking him back. After being miserable for months, he finally met someone, and they hit it off right away. She wasn't as beautiful as Cherise, but she was decent. She was nice, funny, and they had a great time whenever they were together. She was just what he needed, to help him make the transition of getting over Cherise.

And then—out of nowhere, Cherise played a trump, and took him by surprise. He was intrigued by her skills, and didn't just want to walk away from the challenge. If she wanted to play the game, then he was down—he just had to come up with a new strategy.

Yes, he and Cherise had just had sex, and it was good. Yes, he wanted her back, but he also wanted Toni, and had Cherise not been meddling, he would have been able to be with them both—at least until his tour was over—at least eight months down the road. This would give him enough time to really see if Cherise was serious about them getting back together. As far as he knew, she could change her mind at any time, and then where would he be? Alone again?

No matter what he said, Toni wasn't listening. She told him that she didn't believe anything he had to say, and that she didn't want to be with him anymore. He even lowered himself to begging, but that didn't work either. She walked to the door, picked up a bag and handed it to him. She'd packed up everything he'd ever bought her, including the cell phone. After she gave him the bag, she opened the door and asked him to leave.

As he drove away from Toni's house, he became infused with anger towards Cherise. She had no right to stick her nose in his business. If he wanted her to know about Toni, he would have told her. He was so peeved that he'd changed his mind about wanting to be back with her. He didn't want anything to do with her at all. He didn't even want to talk to her, which is why he rejected her last three phone calls. He didn't want to hear her ranting and raving about how she caught him in a lie.

He knew what he had done, and more importantly, he knew why he did it. As far as he was concerned, he didn't owe her any explanation. She got what she deserved, and he didn't feel sorry about it one bit. His only regret was that he hurt Toni in the process. She was innocent in this whole thing, and really didn't deserve any of this. Tomorrow, he would send her flowers, to say how sorry he was. He wouldn't stop until he won her back.

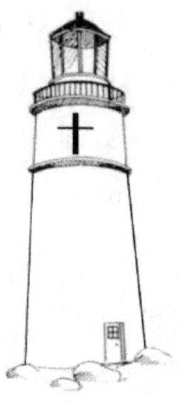

Chapter Twenty-One

The last few days were tough. Cherise would be alright if only Terrell would talk to her. She'd called him several times, every day, but he wouldn't answer her calls. He didn't have any reason to be mad—he was the one who lied. She wasn't sure why she cared, but she did. She wasn't sure why it mattered, but it did. She'd gone weeks without speaking to him, and she was perfectly fine with that, but now, her heart ached at his rejection.

It was a week later when Terrell finally called her back. It was late, and the kids were asleep, but he knew that Cherise would still be up. She never went to bed early, unless she was sick or extremely tired.

Her heart began beating fast when she saw his number on the caller identification device. She was afraid of what he might say, but was quite surprised at the calmness of his tone. When he asked about how she and the girls had been, she could tell that he wasn't as mad as she thought he was. She let out a sigh of relief as she listened attentively to all he had to say.

"I know that I haven't been talking to you, and I want to apologize for cutting you off like that—I was just upset. I also want to apologize for lying to you about Toni. The truth is—she is just a friend.

I should have been honest with you, but I wasn't sure how you would take it since you had just told me that you had forgiven me, and offered to let me come back home. I honestly didn't think that was the right time to tell you, and I really didn't think that it was that important."

This was all that Cherise wanted. A simple apology—Terrell admitting that he was wrong. Now that she was getting what she wanted, she was satisfied. She allowed Terrell to continue speaking—careful not to interrupt.

"This past week, I've had a lot of things on my mind." Pausing between each word, "you…me…us…everything we've been through. We've been together for a long time, and we have really been through a lot. There were some good times though, right?"

"Yes, there were some good times," Cherise answered with a smile.

"Yeah, but I guess the bad times outweighed the good ones, huh?"

Cherise didn't respond, because she didn't want to be the one to speak a negative into a positive situation. She didn't want anything to upset the mood that they were in at this moment. She remained quiet, as Terrell continued...

"I know that I wasn't the best husband, and I know I done a lot of stupid things. I can't say that I know why, because I don't. You are a good person, Cherise, and you didn't deserve the way I treated you. So, for everything—I am truly sorry."

Talk about an apology! This was above and beyond what she expected. She was completely blown away by his words, and her heart danced to the melodies of his heartfelt expressions. With tears of joy falling from her face, she cleared her throat to respond, but was paused when Terrell started back speaking.

"Everyone tried to warn me—you, Pastor Revenew, a few of the members, and oh yeah, the counselor, but I wouldn't listen. Sometimes it's hard to admit when you're wrong, but oh well—I guess it took all this to happen for me to realize how wrong I was.

"I ain't gon' lie, I miss you guys—I really do. I miss y'all so much, and there's not a day that goes by, that I don't think about you. I guess it's true what people say—'you never miss your water til your well runs dry.' I will never be able to say sorry enough, and although I didn't tell you enough, I really did love you, and I still do."

Cherise was speechless. Her mind was saying, "I love you too," but her mouth opened, void of sound. There seemed to have been a block in communication between the two.

"Cherise." The weight of all he had to say was permeating through the sound of his voice, followed by a deep breath. "I don't want to come back home."

Cherise thought she heard him say, he didn't want to come back home, but she knew she'd heard wrong, but just to be sure, she asked, "I'm sorry, what did you say?"

"Cherise, I don't want to come back home. It has nothing to do with another woman or anything like that, but too much has happened, and I just want to close this book."

"Don't you mean chapter?" Cherise asked.

"No. If I close the chapter, I can still go back to the previous chapters, because I'm still in the same book. I don't want to have any memory of this book, and the only way to close this book is—to go through with the divorce."

"Say what?!" Cherise screeched. "Divorce or not, you can't erase the past, and it will always be there. That's just crazy."

"That's your opinion, Cherise. I'm not saying we won't be together in the future, but if we do, it will be in another marriage, not this one."

"Why would you want to waste money on a divorce, and then get remarried later? It would be simple to just try to work it out now, and if it doesn't work, then get the divorce," Cherise pleaded.

"No, Cherise. I don't want to do it that way. I'm going to file for a divorce, because that's what I want."

"Well, what if it's not what I want?"

"That's just too bad. I didn't want to be put out, but I was—against my own will. I didn't want the divorce when you filed, but you didn't ask me my opinion one way or the other. At least I'm letting you know, and not leaving anything to surprise."

"Yeah, but when you asked for me to cancel it, I did. I postponed it to allow time for us to go through counseling, and because of the time, it was automatically cancelled." Frustration was becoming evident in her tone. "You did all that begging to come home, and now that I have agreed to let you come back, you're telling me you don't want to? Last week, you were like okay, but now that I've found out about your little girlfriend, you wanna trip."

"This ain't got nothing to do with Toni," Terrell defended.

"Why didn't you just say that last Sunday?" Before Terrell could respond, she continued to lash out. "Why didn't you say that before you had sex with me?" she yelled.

"Look, Cherise. I'm not going through all this with you. When you made your decision to do what you did—you did what you felt was best for you. Now, I'm doing what I feel is best for me."

Cherise's silence warned Terrell that it was time to end the conversation. Silence for Cherise meant that she was shutting down, and once that happened, it would be a while before she spoke again. Needing an excuse to end the call, Terrell checked his watch, "Look, I gotta go get ready for work. I'll call you later." Still with no response, he pressed the end button on his cell phone, and ended the call.

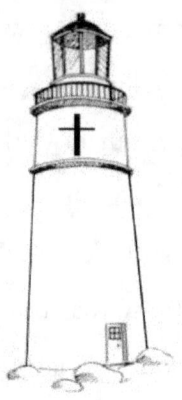

Chapter Twenty-Two

Terrell couldn't have been more wrong—Cherise was definitely surprised. She didn't expect this at all. Had he just told her in the beginning, that he didn't want to come back home, she wouldn't feel so bad. But he went through all that apologizing and professing his love just to say he wanted a divorce.

In a mocking tone, Cherise frowned up her face and spatted, "I don't want to close the chapters, I want to close the book because I don't want to remember the past," repeating what Terrell said to her. "That's the dumbest thing I've ever heard."

Now standing and pacing the floor, Cherise turned her frustration and attention to the Lord. "I didn't ask for this—You wanted this. So, why would You tell me to do something, and then interfere with it? What's the purpose?" The thought of Moses going before Pharoah entered her mind. The Lord told Moses to go back to Egypt and tell Pharoah to let His people go, but then He also told him that He was going to harden Pharoah's heart, so that he wouldn't let the people go.

"At least You prepared Moses, and told him what to expect. At least You told him that you were going to create opposition for him. At least You gave him a warning so that he wasn't caught off guard, but what about me? No warning, no nothing! You just put me out there and made me look like a fool."

"Likewise, ye wives, be in subjection to your own husbands; that, if any obey not the word, they also may without the word be won by the conversation of the wives," the calm voice said. Even though in a whisper, these words spoke louder than Cherise's yelling.

"What does that mean? Why do You keep saying that?" Raising her hands in frustration and then letting them fall down and slap her thighs. "Didn't You just hear that man tell me that he didn't want to come back home, and that he was filing for a divorce? What kind of games are You playing here? Apparently, You're not listening or seeing what's going on down here. What do You want from me?" Cherise yelled out of more frustration.

Feeling helpless and defeated, she laid face down on the bed, and allowed her tears to fall onto her pillow. The weight of her problems rested heavily on her shoulders. Normally she could rely on God for strength, but He was the cause of her sorrow and weakness. He started all of this.

Terrell's words constantly replayed in her head, and with each rerun, her heart ached more. This was one night Cherise was glad that the kids were asleep, so they wouldn't have to witness her pitiful condition. She felt like a supreme pizza, topped with a combination of emotions. Her heart was broken, her pride was hurt, her dignity was crushed and her faith was rocky. She was discouraged by the actions of the Lord, and she was frustrated with His logic.

It was clear to Cherise that the Lord was not going to leave her alone on this matter. He had a way of being a little persistent when He wanted something. She understood exactly how the children of Israel felt. Here was the Lord telling them that He was going to free them, but He actually made things worse for them. Well, maybe, just maybe, as it was with Moses, the Lord had a bigger plan.

Cherise raised back up and sat on the side of the bed. Staring at herself in the mirror on her dresser, she blew a hopeless sigh of defeat. The Lord had won again.

"Lord it doesn't appear that I have a choice in the matter, so I need you to teach me how to go through this assignment. Your Word said that there is nothing new under the sun, so out there, somewhere, there is a woman that has been through this. I need to meet this woman. I need to know how to stand against the opposition. I need to know how she did it."

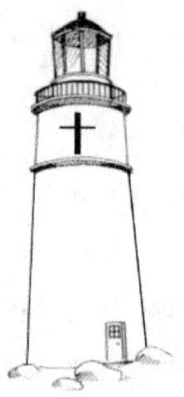

Chapter Twenty-Three

Church had become an almost every day thing for Cherise. It was her way of escape from the thoughts that plagued her mind. If New Harvest didn't have anything going on, she would find a church to go to. Bible study, Friday night services, revivals—you name it, she was there.

While attending different services, she was storing up small nuggets of encouragement and faith that she needed in order to carry on. She noticed that the Lord would often allow her to get real low in spirits, but then He would send a Word of strength, just in the nick of time.

After Bible study one week, Pastor Revenew requested to see Cherise after service. He waited until everyone had left, and he and First Lady sat down, one on each side of Cherise, on the first pew. First Lady didn't really say much, but was mainly there for support.

"What's going on with you?" Pastor Revenew asked Cherise. He'd been noticing a disturbing difference in her for a while. This was not the Cherise he was accustomed to seeing, and he was worried. He finally decided it was time that he talked to her.

"I'm just going through something, and I don't think anyone will understand." Cherise's response was accompanied by a stream of slow tears. She was fine as long as no one asked her any questions, which is why she had been reserved these past few weeks. Normally after services, she would hang around and fellowship with everyone, but lately, immediately after the benediction, she would disappear without a word.

"I'm assuming this has something to do with your marriage, right?"

Cherise shook her head up and down to signify his guess was correct. Just as she was preparing to wipe her tears away with her hands, First Lady Revenew offered her some tissues she had gotten from the Kleenex box sitting on the end of the pew.

"We can tell that something has been troubling you. We've been concerned, and wanted to know if there was anything we could do for you."

"I don't think there's anything anyone can do. I tried so hard to stay in my marriage as long as I could. I put up with all kinds of crap for the sake of being saved and being a minister. I did my best not to let God down."

First Lady Revenew saw Cherise's pain, and rubbed her on the back to comfort her, as she continued to release her feelings, "Then when I finally had enough, I filed for a divorce. Then, trying to be nice and look out for other people's feelings, I put the divorce on hold and tried counseling and that didn't work. I was completely done with everything. I was happy and content with me and my girls," Cherise continued.

"All of a sudden, here comes God messing with me about taking Terrell back. I wasn't trying to listen to that, but He wouldn't let it go, and when you preached on forgiveness that Sunday, that confirmed it. So I went to Terrell and told him that I forgive him, and told him that he could come back home, and guess what? He didn't want to come back home. Now, he wants a divorce. But I know what God told me, so I just don't understand," Cherise cried.

"Let me ask you this. What do you want? Now wait before you answer. I want you to listen to me real good. I want you to think real hard before you answer. I want you to tell me, at the end, after everything is said and done, what do you want the end result to be?" Pastor Revenew asked.

"I want my marriage to be restored," Cherise answered as she looked back and forth at the pastor and his wife.

"Hmmm . . . Are you sure? I mean are you absolutely, positively sure that's what you want?"

Cherise didn't show it, but she was tickled at Pastor Revenew's deep expression on his face as he asked his last question. "Yes," she answered boldly.

"Okay. I want you to listen to me. I want to teach you something about faith." He looked at Cherise to make sure he had her undivided attention. "Let me show you what faith can do. God created the world with faith. He created something out of nothing with only the words He spoke. Faith is sooo powerful that it can make a person do something that they've declared they would never do. To some that don't understand it, it may look like witchcraft, but it's not—it's faith. Do you understand me so far?"

Cherise shook her head up and down again to indicate she understood.

"I have to ask because I don't want you to misunderstand what it is that I'm actually saying. I need you to understand that, if God can speak to nothing and create something, then you can speak to nothing and create something. Just because your husband said that he's not coming back home, doesn't mean that he won't come back home. Just because he wants a divorce, doesn't mean you have to get a divorce.

"The Bible says, 'according to your faith, be it done to you.' What does that mean? That means *you* are in control of your own faith. You can believe big, or you can believe small, but you can have whatever you say if you," pointing his finger at Cherise, "believe . . . that . . . you . . . will . . . have . . . what . . . you . . . say."

Pastor Revenew grabbed Cherise by the hand, "This is what I want you to do—every morning when you wake up, I want you to say…Lord, I thank you for restoring my marriage. Every time Terrell says he's not coming home, I want you to say… Lord, I thank you for restoring my marriage. Whenever it seems like your marriage is not going to be restored, I want you to say . . . Lord, I thank you for restoring my marriage. No matter how bad it gets, no matter what it looks like—because I can assure you that the enemy is going to do his best to make you give up. It's gonna be hard, but no matter how hard it gets,

don't you turn from your confession—you say, no matter what
. . . Lord, I thank you for restoring my marriage. If you can
believe that He can do it, then He will do it. According to your
faith, be it done unto you."

Cherise felt like Pastor Revenew had just performed a
spoken word piece. It was so deep and refreshing. Had they
been in a poetry setting, she would snap her fingers to show
her appreciation for his work, but since they were not, she
reached out and gave him the biggest hug she could offer.
When she released the pastor, she turned and gave First Lady
Revenew an even bigger hug. Although First Lady Revenew
didn't say anything with her mouth, Cherise heard her actions
clearly.

Everything was coming together for Cherise. First Lady's
actions had just opened her eyes to the scripture God had been
whispering to her. If she was going to win Terrell back, it
wouldn't be with her words, but by her actions—for her
actions would speak louder than anything she had to say.

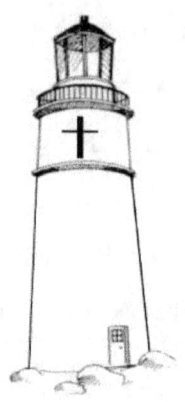

Chapter Twenty-Four

"*For we wrestle not against flesh and blood, but against principalities, against powers, against the rulers of the darkness of this world, against spiritual wickedness in high places,*" the guest speaker at House of Deliverance, Church of God in Christ, quoted the scripture from Ephesians, six and twelve. They were having a revival and Cherise had planned to attend as many nights as she could, without taking her away from her responsibilities at New Harvest.

She had been faithfully confessing, "Lord, I thank you for restoring my marriage," every day for a couple of weeks now, but she still wasn't seeing any results. Terrell was still messing with Toni and still talking about filing for the divorce, but she held on to everything Pastor Revenew told her.

The minister entitled his message, "Know Who You're Fighting." Cherise took notes as she learned that the real enemy in her battle was not her husband, but Satan. Even though Terrell was the one that spoke hurtful words and did hurtful things, the one who lied, the one who was having an affair, and the one who she argued with—he was not the real enemy.

She learned that it was important to know who the real enemy was, in order to know how to fight. You can't fight him, if you can't identify him. Being that Satan is a spirit, she couldn't fight him in the flesh. She learned that she couldn't fight spiritual things with carnal things. Her weapons were not powerful enough and would not work.

The following night, Cherise received her next nugget when the guest speaker quoted Mark, eleven and twenty-three, "For verily I say unto you, that whosoever shall say unto this mountain, be thou removed, and be thou cast into the sea; and shall not doubt in his heart, but shall believe that those things which he saith shall come to pass; he shall have whatsoever he saith." This time the message was titled, "You Will Have Whatsoever You Say."

Cherise could hardly contain herself as the minister explained the difference between a person with weak faith and a person with strong faith. "Faith and trust go hand in hand, when you're believing God to do the impossible. It's one thing to have weak faith, and it's another thing to have strong faith. What and how you believe makes all the difference in the world when you're going through.

"Weak faith says, I believe God can do this...I believe God can heal me...I believe God can deliver me...I believe God can restore my marriage...I believe God can bring me out of this situation, but when faith has been tried, it develops something in you, and your weak faith becomes strong faith. This is called trust, which says—I KNOW God WILL do this...I KNOW God WILL heal me...I KNOW God WILL deliver me...I KNOW God WILL restore my marriage...I KNOW God WILL bring me out of this situation."

The preacher's excitement was demonstrated through his animated voices and dramatic illustrations, as well as the way he ran from one end of the pulpit to the other. He was very persuasive as he ministered from his own trying experiences. The congregation was full of people standing and shouting as the minister's message activated their faith to another level.

"Yes, God can do it, but will he? Only you can answer that question, according to what you believe. Do you believe that He can? Or do you believe that He will?" the exhausted minister questioned.

Cherise was encouraged. She felt like she had taken a magical potion that gave her special powers to overcome anything. Each sermon that was preached was nourishment to her hungry soul.

Her flesh was weak, but her spirit was indeed strong. She hadn't been able to eat much of anything for the past two weeks. She tried, but the Lord wouldn't let her. She would make plans with Sasha and Sybill to go out for lunch, but right before the time came to go, she would cancel. She had no appetite for food whatsoever.

Every day during lunch, she would sit in her car listening to pre-recorded sermons or music, pray and read the Bible. It got so bad that Sasha stopped asking, "What do you want to do for lunch today?" and started asking, "Are you eating lunch today?" Sasha tried to be supportive of Cherise as much as she could, but she was starting to get worried.

Sybill wasn't quite as understanding, and because of her ignorance to spiritual things, she would often throw jabs of insult at Cherise for putting herself through such self-inflicted pain. She really wasn't trying to be mean, but she didn't like seeing Cherise hurting and all this suffering for a man who didn't want to be with her was just crazy. Sybill couldn't believe that God would want anybody to put up with, or remain in a horrible marriage, such as Cherise and Terrell's.

Although Cherise was hurt by Sybill's words and actions, she understood. It was not easy to sit back and watch somebody you love hurt, and not be able to do anything about it. As much as Cherise wished both, Sybill and Sasha could relate to her situation at the moment, they couldn't.

Cherise began to withdraw herself as much as possible from her friends in order to stay focused on her trial. She loved them, but she couldn't allow any negativity whatsoever, to distract her, nor could she allow any doubt from them to taint her faith.

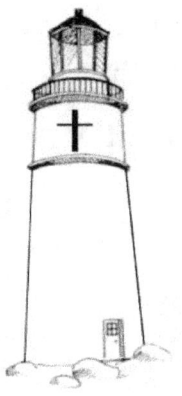

Chapter Twenty-Five

Cherise sat at her desk, and read an email from one of her team members about an irate customer that she needed to call. She dreaded calling the customer back because she wasn't in the mood for all the bickering and complaining. She was prepared to give the lady whatever she wanted to appease her in order to make both of their days less stressful. She closed her eyes and sent up a simple prayer before dialing the customer's number.

Lauren Brooks lived in Bakersfield, California and had been separated and standing for her marriage for about two months. Her husband, Jeff, decided to leave her on Christmas day. She'd been away at her aunt's for Christmas Eve, with her parents, and was anxious to get back home to spend Christmas with her husband. He called her, literally, every twenty minutes to tell her that he loved her. If he told her once, he told her at least a hundred times—but there was something different in his voice that demanded her attention. The words, "I love you" had never felt so scary.

When she arrived home, she was disappointed to see that Jeff's car wasn't in the driveway. Lauren was excited, and couldn't wait to surprise him with the gift she had purchased for him. She expected him to be at the door, waiting to greet her with a hug and a kiss. It hadn't been that long since she'd spoken to him on the phone, and he assured her he would be there when she arrived.

Before getting out of the car, she called him to see where he was, and when he would return home. While talking to him, she could tell by his stalling that something wasn't right. Trying her best to contain her anger, she yelled at him and demanded he tell her what was wrong. He finally released the words, "I'm not coming back home. I'm leaving you, Lauren."

Lauren immediately panicked at his words, and begged him not to do this. "It's Christmas," she cried. Christmas was supposed to be happy, and exciting. She loved surprises, but this gift was not on her Christmas list.

Jeff told Lauren he'd left her a letter in the house that would explain everything, along with five hundred dollars to help with the next month's bills. She held him on the phone until she had found it, and cried as she read the painful separation notice. Jeff had listed in detail, the undeniable truths as to why he was leaving.

Lauren had two sickly parents that demanded the majority of her attention. Amongst the stress, the couple's relationship had gotten rocky, and they argued all the time. Out of anger, Lauren would often remove her wedding ring, and Jeff had warned her to stop doing it. She wasn't proud of it, but there were a few times when she reacted in a rage, and Jeff had finally reached his breaking point.

After the breakup, for almost a week, with the exception of taking care of the needs of her parents, Lauren stayed in bed. She didn't have any desire to live anymore, and had prayed on several occasions that she wouldn't wake up. The pain was worse than anything she had ever felt before, and the thought of suicide seemed like a good idea.

As she contemplated whether to take the bottle of pills she held in her hand, the preacher on the Trinity Broadcasting Network began to minister to her. If she didn't know any better, she would have thought he could see her and what she was about to do through the television screen. He told her that God loved her, and when she didn't have any hope, he gave her hope. As she got out of bed, and placed her hand on the screen, as instructed by the unknown preacher, he spoke words of life back into her, and gave her the desire to live again.

A few weeks later, Lauren called the phone company where Cherise worked to discuss a problem with her bill. Due to a misunderstanding with the customer service representative that answered her call, she requested a manager to call her back. When Cherise returned the call, one conversation led to another, and before it was all over, even though it was against company policies, Lauren and Cherise had exchanged numbers.

Cherise's prayers had been answered above what she asked for. She requested to meet someone whom had walked this walk before, but He gave her someone that was walking it at the same time she was. They talked daily about their situations, and became each other's accountability partner. They would cry together, rejoice together, fast together, laugh together, and every day, they would pray together.

They prayed for each other's faith and strength. They prayed for each other's marriages to be restored. They prayed for each other's husbands—that the Lord would not allow the enemy to devour them. They prayed for the other women involved—that the Lord would remove them out of their husband's lives, but also that He would bless and save them.

Along with prayer, Lauren and Cherise began to diligently study the Word for their situation. They were like kids during an Easter egg hunt—each time they found an egg, they became more and more excited and wanted to find more. Soon, they began taking their focus off their husbands, and allowed the Lord to purge and teach them how to be Godly wives and wise women. They learned many things about marriage God's way, but the main thing that stood out was the lesson in forgiveness.

They learned that although God allowed Moses to permit divorce for the hardness of the people's hearts, that hard hearts were actually a form of un-forgiveness, which still had to be dealt with eventually. Forgiveness was necessary in order to stay in right standing with God. The truth was, whether the marriages were restored or not, if Lauren and Cherise didn't forgive Jeff and Terrell, they couldn't expect God to forgive them.

Cherise thought back to when she was seeking for scriptures to justify her leaving Terrell, she could hardly find any, but now that she was studying scriptures, seeking for restoration, she had more than she could count. This was just another example of God's redemptive love. The way she saw it, God was more about restoring, resurrecting, reviving and redeeming than he was about giving up on people and situations that seemed to be a lost cause.

She learned that even in adultery, God was not giving people a reason to divorce, but a chance to show forth unconditional love and forgiveness. That even in a separation, not to first seek divorce, but instead, restoration. He doesn't expect everybody to give up. Somebody has to stand. Somebody has to fight. Somebody has to try. Somebody has to forgive.

Cherise thought about the traditional wedding vows—*I take you to be my wedded husband, to have and to hold, from this day forward, for better, for worse, for richer, for poorer, in sickness and in health, to love and to cherish, till death do us part.*

She had never really paid any real attention to the vows in detail before. The words, WORSE, POORER, SICKNESS— stood out like never before. Just as there is a positive, there is the possibility of a negative. She realized that most people who get married say the vows, but don't really mean the vows. They don't plan on—worse, poorer, or sickness, they only expect—better, richer, and health.

Cherise could see herself being an advocate for marriages. The thought of writing a book pressed heavily upon her heart. She was beginning to desire to see not only hers, but other marriages saved, and those that were separated—restored. She believed that no matter the situation, if allowed, there was no situation too hard for God.

She knew that there would be others standing for their marriages, and they would need an example to look to. She was willing to be that example. She took notes and studied even the more. She envisioned herself doing seminars and workshops for all—those married and those seeking to be married one day.

With her right hand clutching the cross around her neck, she professed, "Lord, if you restore my marriage, I will never withhold your goodness, but will proclaim it from the mountaintop. I will preach and teach your word. I will do your will."

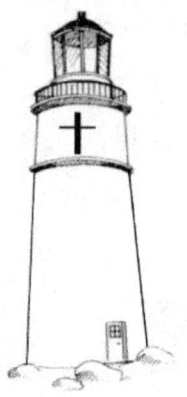

Chapter Twenty-Six

The kids were spending the weekend with their grandparents, and Cherise was left alone—physically, mentally, and emotionally. The solitude was beginning to take a toll on her, and she felt like she was about to lose her mind. The things that she was experiencing were unheard of, and even if she told someone, they wouldn't understand. She didn't understand for that matter.

She had spent hours trying to fall asleep, and was suddenly awakened by an eerie feeling. Helplessly, Cherise cried as she tried, but couldn't get out of the bed. She was sick, and what she was feeling was torture to her soul. She could literally feel the intimacy between Terrell and the other woman.

She rolled from side to side moaning and begging God to relieve her from this feeling. Talk about reliving a moment—the last time she felt pain like this, she was naked, on the floor in her bathroom, seeking deliverance from Terrell. Now, she was seeking restoration for her marriage to Terrell. It would be easier just to walk away.

Everything she was enduring was completely against her own will. For a brief moment, she regretted saying the words, "not my will, but yours Lord." She wanted to renege on her promise. This was more than she bargained for. It was one thing for the enemy to play with her mind, but this was ridiculous. She didn't even want to think about Terrell being with another woman, let alone feel him being with one.

Remembering the agony Jesus endured in the Garden of Gethsemane, she imagined what He must have felt like when his sweat resembled drops of blood. How severe was His anguish? Whatever he felt, she was sure it was still more severe than what she was feeling.

Encouraged by His strength to endure, she surrendered everything unto the Lord. She did the only thing she knew to do—she prayed as Jesus prayed yet again, "not my will Lord, but yours." Searching for strength, she repeatedly called in a whisper, "Jesus, Jesus, Jesus." She wept until the feeling ceased, and fell asleep cuddling one of her pillows.

*****

The alarm sounded, signaling that it was time to pray. Cherise was drained due to the real life nightmare she had just experienced. She slid out of the bed onto the floor in a praying position with her head remaining on the bed. She didn't want to appear lazy before the Lord, but she couldn't muster up enough energy to worry about correct posture. She prayed a short prayer, thanked the Lord for her marriage being restored again, and crawled back in the bed.

When Cherise finally awoke, it was almost noon. She was still exhausted because—although she had slept for many hours, she didn't get any rest. Her mind was having a mind of its own, and although she was asleep, her mind was very much wide awake. She stared at the clock for minutes before dragging herself out of bed. She sluggishly walked to the bathroom, and when she had finished, she looked in the mirror as she washed her hands.

"Lord, thank you for restoring my marriage," she spoke but was quickly taken aback.

Cherise was deeply disturbed, and frowned at her reflection. *Oh my God. No wonder everyone seemed so worried.* She stroked her face with her hands, and then ran her fingers through her hair, and inspected the brittle ends. *They must have thought I was sick or something.* This ordeal had taken a serious toll on her, and she looked terrible. She had lost weight, and the constant pulling of her hair back into a ponytail had broken off her edges.

She normally didn't wear ponytails often because Terrell said that wearing them was an easy way for a woman to cover up if she was messing around. With ponytails, she didn't have to worry about her hair messing up, or taking a long time trying to fix it back. Though that was one of the stupidest things she'd ever heard, it was easier just to not wear them and keep the peace.

It was at that moment that she decided she needed to pull herself together. If she was going to go through this thing, whatever it was, with the Lord, she couldn't do it looking like this. She had an image to uphold, and right now, she was looking a hot mess.

Cherise called her childhood friend and hairstylist, Shatega, and asked if she could squeeze her in. She knew that Saturdays were Shatega's busiest day, but she would pay double if she had to. She just couldn't go one more day looking like this.

After Shatega had scolded her for not taking care of her hair, and made her beautiful again, Cherise forced herself to get dressed. She'd been invited to dinner with Sasha, Sybill, and their husbands. It had been awhile since she'd really hung out with them, and she wasn't trying to dismiss her friends altogether. She just needed time apart to build her strength to fight this battle of faith.

They agreed to meet at the restaurant around 6 o'clock that evening, and the time was quickly approaching. She didn't want to be a third wheel, well a fifth one in this case—but she needed relief for her mind.

As they entered the doors of the restaurant, they were greeted by the maitre'd.

"Good afternoon. How many will be dining?"

"Five," everyone said, with the exception of Cherise.

"Six," Cherise objected.

Everyone looked at Cherise, confused. What was she talking about? Everyone, including the hostess, looked around and recounted everyone in the party.

"Will someone be joining you later?" the gentleman asked, looking at Cherise. He assumed her date would be coming in later.

"No, he's already here," Cherise said with a straight face. She could see that everyone was confused, so she explained. "I'm speaking those things that be not as though they were. So although y'all don't see him, he's here."

"You crazy," Sybill said, while shaking her head in disagreement. Cherise totally agreed with Sybill—she was crazy. She felt crazy when she said it, because it was clearly only five people in their party—however, this was one time she was willing to look, or even be crazy, if this is what having crazy faith meant.

Still confused, the hostess shrugged his shoulders, and decided to play along. He grabbed six menus, and led them to their table. As he walked away, the young bubbly waitress came and stood before them.

"Hi. My name is Alicia, and I will be your waitress for the evening. May I take your drink orders?"

Everyone greeted Alicia with their hellos, and individually gave their choice of beverage. Cherise ordered two waters— one for her, and one for Terrell. The waitress took their orders without asking any questions, assuming that the guest for the empty chair would be joining them soon.

"I'll give you a few minutes to look over your menus, while I get your drinks."

At first, everyone was unsure how to handle Cherise and her strange behavior, but by the time they had eaten, they were all laughing with her, instead of at her. Sasha and her husband were church goers, and although they had never had to believe God to such a magnitude before, they knew all about faith, and what it meant to have it. Sasha was just happy to see her friend eating, and having a good time.

Sybill on the other hand, thought that everything Cherise was doing for the sake of her marriage was just plain stupid. She didn't agree with the whole "standing for your marriage" ordeal at all. She couldn't see why anyone would want to make herself look crazy in front of others.

Sybill's husband however, was more optimistic. He always had a positive attitude. He didn't know much about spiritual things either, but it excited him to watch Cherise act out what she believed. Never had he seen this type of faith before. He didn't know if it was going to work, but he was secretly cheering for her to win her battle.

They spent the rest of the evening, enjoying each other's company, and every now and then, someone would make a funny about the absent, but present Terrell. They would say things like, "Terrell how's your dinner?" or "Terrell, you've been awful quiet tonight, is everything alright?" Then after everyone had eaten, paid their bill, and walked outside preparing to leave, they all bid Terrell, "goodnight," with the exception of Sybill.

Cherise found her friends, and their jokes to be quite comical. Even though she was the laugh of the party, this was just what she needed, to get her mind off her problems—even if it was only for a few hours.

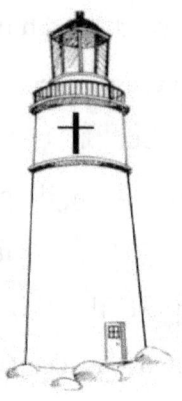

Chapter Twenty-Seven

On the way home from the restaurant, Cherise's phone went off. She hoped it was Terrell, but the number didn't look familiar. Just in case he was calling from work, she decided to answer it any way.

"Hello"

"Hey beautiful."

She couldn't believe it. She knew that voice anywhere.

"Mario?" she questioned.

It had been almost a year since she had last spoken to Mario. The phone company was forced to do cutbacks, and his job was one of the ones that were eliminated. Shortly after, he moved away to Burlington, North Carolina for another job opportunity.

Although she was sad to see him go, she couldn't help but feel that God orchestrated it. After the incident with the sex demon, she tried her best to avoid contact with him, but with Mario being the mailroom guy—that was kind of hard to do. This was God's way of providing a way for her to escape the temptation of being with Mario—out of sight, out of mind.

It was strange that he would call her on a Saturday, this late in the evening. Even when he lived in Georgia, he had never done that before. She hadn't told him that she and Terrell were separated, so how would he know it was safe to call.

"Cherise," Mario called.

"Oh…I'm sorry. I was just caught off guard. I know I didn't recognize the number, but I didn't expect it to be you."

"Well don't sound so excited," he joked.

Cherise smiled. "I didn't mean it like that." Mario always had a way of making her smile.

"Sure you didn't," he continued joking with her.

"Aw hush. I'm always happy to hear from you. How have you been?"

"Pretty good. How 'bout you? How have you been?"

She didn't want to tell him the real truth—that she had been going through hell, and that some days, she was close to losing her mind, so she decided to go with the normal response.

"I'm fine."

"Well I know that," he teased. "I actually just saw you leaving the restaurant. I didn't see anyone in the car with you, so I took the chance on calling you."

"Really?" she squeaked with excitement. "I didn't know you were in town."

"Yeah, I came to visit my mom for the weekend."

"Oh okay. I didn't see you at the restaurant."

"No, I was just passing by, and luckily I was stopped by the red light. I was happy to see you, even if was from afar."

"Aww, isn't that sweet."

"Yeah, right. It's funny too, because you've been on my mind all day."

Cherise smiled at the thought of someone thinking about her. Not only was she feeling lonely, she didn't feel attractive much either.

"Oh yeah… What have you been thinking about?"

"Trust me, you don't want to know."

"Yes I do. Tell me."

"You sure?"

"Yeah, tell me."

"Naaaaw, I better not," Mario said with hesitation.

"Aw, come on and tell me. You shouldn't have said nothing." Curiosity was getting the best of her.

"Okay, you asked." He took a deep breath, and said, "I've been thinking about tasting your banana split."

Cherise almost went off the road. They've played sex games before, but she wasn't prepared for his statement. She didn't know what she expected to hear, but that definitely wasn't it. His words caused an exciting sexual desire to arise within her body.

"Boy, stop playing like that. You shouldn't say things like that, because you make me…"

"You asked," he said before she could finish her sentence. "What you're feeling right now is just a few rain drops, but I want to cause a tsunami."

A tsunami? Dang, I've never felt a tsunami before. Right then, everything in her flesh wanted to know what a tsunami felt like. The timing couldn't have been more perfect. The kids were away at their grandparents, and although Terrell was with her at the restaurant, he wasn't with her now. In fact, he was probably somewhere with Toni anyway.

"Why would you be thinking something like that?"

"Actually, I was looking through my phone and I ran across your picture you sent me. Sometimes when I get lonely, I look at it."

Cherise didn't have to ask what picture, because she knew exactly what picture he was talking about. She wasn't proud of it, but one night after Terrell had fallen asleep; she took a picture of her most sacred body part, and sent it to him through text message. He had done the same thing, but after she had started encountering the incubus spirit, she quickly deleted it. She didn't admit it to Pastor Revenew, but she knew this was the key that opened the door for the incubus spirit to come into her life.

"You need to throw that thing away, Mario," she said with a disgusted frown on her face. She regretted that she had allowed herself to slip up and do something so repugnant. This was totally out of character for her. She felt like Steve Urkel when he would say his famous line, "Oops...Did I do thaaat?" She couldn't believe herself.

"Whyyyyy?" Mario whined.

"Because I said so," she snapped.

He could tell that Cherise was serious by her tone, and without a fight, he simply said, "Okay."

"I'm serious."

"I can tell, so I promise I will delete it. Now, are you gonna let me taste your banana split?"

His offer was hard to turn down. Although she wasn't the one that would be eating the banana split, she was sure she would enjoy watching him do the honors. Just the thought alone was delicious.

"Umm... I don't think that's a good idea."

"Pleeeaaaase," he begged.

"Quit it Mario."

"Alright, alright... I don't want to pressure you, but I would really love to see you. Can you at least let me see you before I leave in the morning? We don't have to do anything, I promise."

"You just saw me."

"Oh, you got jokes. That's not the same thing, and you know it."

"I know, I know," she laughed. "As much as I would like to, I can't do it right now, but maybe later. Is this your new number? I will save it, and if I can meet you later, I'll call you."

"Yeah, this is my number. Are you for real?"

"What did I say?"

"Alright, alright. Don't lie to me now."

"Okay, now bye."

"I'll be waiting."

"Bye, Mario."

"Alright, later."

Cherise prayed all the way home. Her flesh was warring with her spirit, and the flesh was giving the spirit a run for its money. It didn't take her long to realize that the devil was the culprit. It was his job to make her fall by any means necessary, and he knew exactly what, well, in this case, *who* to tempt her with. She was learning everyday what it meant to not fall ignorant to the devil's devices. She had to stay prayed up and guarded at all times.

After entering the house, she went straight to the bathroom and took a shower. Before she could dry off, Mario was calling her phone, but she refused to answer. She was no fool. She knew that if she went to meet Mario, she would be in his bed before they could count to ten.

When the voicemail indicator appeared on her phone, she pressed the power button and turned the phone completely off. As much as she wanted to feel a tsunami, she was determined not to let the enemy win tonight. It would be all over in the morning—Mario would be leaving town.

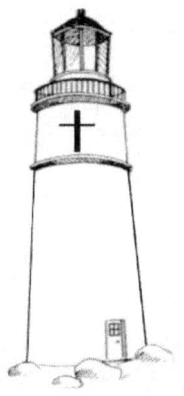

Chapter Twenty-Eight

Sleep was at its best as the raindrops played soothing rhythms against the window pane. Cherise's body rested against the strong frame that perfectly cupped around her body. Just like a jigsaw puzzle, his body fit snuggly against hers, interlocking to resemble one.

Neither one of them wanted to move to answer the doorbell that had interrupted the peaceful melodies of the rain, but since it was her house, it was best she responded to the call. She regretfully loosed her body from his grip, and rolled out of the bed. She removed her robe from the bed post, wrapped it around her body, and walked towards the living room.

Before opening the door, she noticed by the clock on the DVD player, that it was not quite six a.m. She frowned because she would have had a few more minutes to sleep before having to get ready for work. *Who could this be at this time of morning?*

"Who is it?"

She couldn't hear the response over the rain, so she cracked the door to see who was on the other side.

"Good Morning, Ma'am? Are you Cherise Tillman?" The officer asked.

Confused with a twist of fear, she responded "Yes. How may I help you?"

"I'm sorry to wake you, but this is for you." The officer held out his hand that revealed a sealed envelope.

"What is it?"

"I'm not sure ma'am. I just deliver them."

Hesitantly, she took the envelope and offered, "Thank you."

"Have a nice day."

"You too."

Curious, Cherise turned on the lamp to see what was inside the envelope. She tore open the package and began reading the contents inside. She couldn't believe her eyes. Terrell had actually filed for a divorce.

What the...? Cherise had to catch herself. She knew what Pastor Revenew had taught her to say, but she couldn't find those words of thanks at the moment. This was an awkward situation because, while she was in the living room tripping over the divorce papers, the man she allowed to please her last night was still lying in her bed.

Ever since Mario had come to town, she had been feeling pretty vulnerable. His sexual offers weakened her flesh and the desire to make love and be loved had been magnified more than normal. At this point, it didn't take much to get her in bed and she had allowed herself to fall prey to her own vulnerabilities.

Cherise tipped in her room and turned on the lights. She felt a knot in the pit of her belly as she watched the still body resting peacefully in her bed. Like an explosive bomb, Cherise snatched the covers back and exposed Terrell's naked body. How dare he lay in her bed night after night acting like everything was okay—knowing good and well what he had done.

Her first thought was to go in the kitchen, start a pot of grits, and once they were good and popping hot, give him a little taste of what Al Green felt. Her second thought was to go Lorena Bobbitt on him. She quickly dismissed the two prior thoughts, because she was sane enough to know she couldn't do any jail time. Praying would have been the appropriate thing to do for a Christian, but how could she pray with the kinds of thoughts running through her mind. As much as she tried not to, she couldn't press her lips together tight enough, to keep the profane language from escaping.

She knew that he had mentioned wanting a divorce, but since he had been coming around more, spending time with them, she thought that maybe he had changed his mind. She just assumed that things were getting better. Cherise thought that God was honoring her prayers, and rewarding her fasting, or maybe it was the bold faith she exemplified in front of her friends that got His attention and gave her extra kudos.

She had been praying for open doors and opportunities to bless her husband, so if he needed a cooked meal—she did it and thanked the Lord for the opportunity. If he needed his clothes washed—she did them and thanked the Lord for the opportunity. If he needed sex—she put on her best performances and thanked the Lord for the opportunity. The more she stayed humbled and non-confrontational, the more she could see things changing in her favor—the more she could see her marriage being restored.

"Divorce?! You have the nerve to be coming around here like everything is okay, sleep with me and still have me served with some freaking divorce papers?" she yelled.

"Cherise, calm down and quit acting crazy before you wake up them kids." Terrell jumped up out the bed and grabbed his pants to put on. "I don't know what you're so upset for, because I told you I was filing for a divorce over a month ago. Ain't nothing changed."

"If nothing's changed, why have you been coming around, acting like everything was okay? Why have you been letting me do all this stuff for you, including having sex with you, if you knew you were still wanting a divorce? Do you think I was doing these things for my health?" She was still yelling, but about two octaves lower than before.

"If I knew you were going to act like this, I would have never started back messing around with you. I figured you were fine with it."

"Lies! You're telling lies, Terrell. You know darn well I was not fine with you sleeping with me every night you were in town, and still filing for a divorce. Anytime you mentioned anything about a divorce, I told you that I didn't want one."

"Like I said, nothing's changed. I told you I wanted a divorce, and that's what I'm going to get."

"No…what you can get is—your stuff and GET OUT OF MY HOUSE."

"Are you serious? It's raining cats and dogs out there."

"Good. You should feel right at home, because that's what you are—a freaking dog."

Once again, Cherise felt used and betrayed—but it was her own fault for assuming. Just because they had slept together during a moment of passion last month after Alysa's birthday party, didn't give her a reason to assume they were working things out, and it wasn't. It was the fact that every day since that day, Terrell was calling her more, texting her more, and whenever he was in town, he was sleeping over. They never discussed it, but it just seemed like it was understood, based on the way things were progressing. Guess the old saying was true—when you assume, you make a, you know what out of yourself.

Cherise was too stubborn to let Terrell see her breakdown and cry. She wouldn't even give him the satisfaction of knowing how deeply hurt she was, but as soon as he left, she sobbed sorely. As hard as it was to muster up the words, she cried, "Lord, thank you for restoring my marriage."

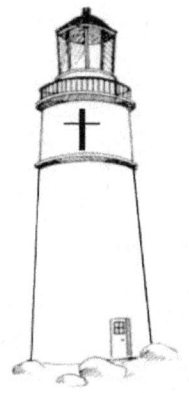

Chapter Twenty-Nine

"Lord, thank you for restoring my marriage," Cherise confessed as she tried to fight the thoughts that plagued her mind. The devil was torturing her by playing annoying scenes of another woman with her husband. Some were sexual, but the majority was scenes of the perfect couple in love.

Terrell don't want you. Even when he's with you, he's thinking about her. He don't love you, he loves her. That's why he wants a divorce—so he can marry her.

"Lord, thank you for restoring my marriage."

You can confess all you want, he's not coming back. He don't love you, he loves her. He loves being with her, kissing her, making love to her.

"Will you shut up?" Cherise yelled. She was sure the other drivers on the highway thought she was crazy by the way she was carrying on. She even tried turning up the volume of the music playing on her CD, but that didn't work either.

See how you're acting. That's why Terrell doesn't want you. You're pathetic. He's never coming back. He loves Toni. He wants Toni. He wants to be with Toni.

She knew Toni was still in the picture, but when Terrell started calling and coming around more, she didn't pose as much of a threat as she did when Cherise first found out about her. Now that she'd been served with divorce papers, Toni was all she could think about . . . *Toni is going to have your husband. Toni is going to make your husband leave you. Toni is going to do things to please your husband that you could never do. As a matter of fact, Toni's making love to your husband right now. Toni is better than you. Toni, Toni, Toni...*

"Lord, you sure do think a lot of me. You must think I'm pretty strong, huh? You said that you would never put no more on me than I can bear, and I swear I can't handle this, but apparently you do, otherwise you wouldn't have chosen me, huh?" Cherise asked, and looked up as if she was waiting on an answer.

Cherise wanted to scream, but she laughed to keep from crying. She remembered her mother telling her how the enemy likes to play with the mind, and if at any time she needed to stop the thoughts he was bringing, all she had to do was sing out loud, and the thoughts would stop. She said that the mind couldn't do both at the same time.

Cherise began to sing, "I neeeeeeed thee ooooooooooooh, I need theeee. Ev—ry hoooour, I neeeeed theeee. Bless me now my Sa—vior, I come tooooo to thee."

Cherise was amazed that it worked. The devil was really having his way with her mind, but sure enough, whenever she would sing, the thoughts would stop. After going back and forth a few times, eventually the torturing thoughts ceased for a while.

Cherise always joked with her mom, that she wasn't a normal mother or grandmother. She didn't cook, bake or even babysit that much, but she could always count on her to provide sound advice when it came to things of life—naturally and spiritually.

Virginia Stanford had Cherise when she was only fourteen. She was still a child herself, so Cherise was more like a

playmate than a daughter. Cherise's father had sex with
Virginia against her will, but she in turn ended up marrying
him in order to please her parents. Her relationship with
Cherise's father was rather abusive, and after she escaped, she
found the Lord and tried to rebuild the life that was taken
from her at such an early age.

Virginia had gone through a lot growing up, but she didn't
look her age nor did she look anything like what she had gone
through. For a grandmother, she was fine. She had a small
waist line and a big ol' booty. Cherise often teased her by
changing the lyrics of E.U.'s ole school classic "Da' Butt" to,
"Virginia got a big ole butt (oh, yeah)." Not only was Virginia
fine, but she loved to be stylish and she was free in her
sexuality. Being saved didn't mean you couldn't be sexy and
look good.

As she grew in the Lord, she and Cherise became very
close. Not only did their relationship evolve as mother and
daughter, they also became close friends. They could talk
about any and every thing, and just like today, she could always
count on her mother's wisdom and knowledge to get her
through.

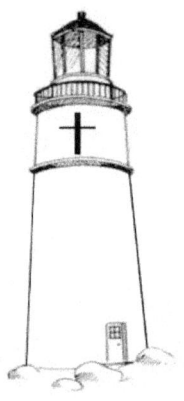

Chapter Thirty

Cherise didn't have any extra money to fight the divorce, so she had to rely on the Lord to be her attorney. Besides, she remembered that Attorney Montgomery told her that fighting a divorce only prolongs it, but it doesn't stop the divorce from actually going through. Basically, a person can't make someone stay married to them, if that person really wants to divorce. It would be a waste of time and money.

Cherise did everything that she was required to do, except sign the divorce papers. Today she was scheduled for a Divorce Parenting Class that was required in the state of Georgia before a divorce could be finalized. She had the option to attend a class at the same time as Terrell or attend one by herself. Since she was prolonging, Terrell went ahead and got his class out the way. She held off as long as she could, but against her own will, she had to finally attend the class.

As she sat in the room filled with people getting divorced, her heart ached. She wondered what were their reasons, and if they had even tried to work it out. Did they try counseling? Did both parties want the divorce? Was anyone fighting to save the marriage? Was there anyone feeling the way she was feeling? Was anyone seeking restoration, despite what the one filing for the divorce says?

As she sat in the two hour class, listening to the facilitator teach the do's and don'ts of a divorced parent, she bowed her head. She wanted to stand and beg the people to reconsider their decision to divorce. She was sure that some of the marriages could be saved, if only she could talk to them. However, that was not what she was there to do, so she sat quietly and prayed. She prayed for everyone in the room, and of course, she thanked the Lord for restoring her marriage.

After the course, she received her certification of completion like it was something she was supposed to be proud of. It wasn't like she was going to hang it up in a frame for all her guests to see. Instead, she took it home and filed it away so that she didn't have to look at it, or think about what it represented.

After she and the girls had eaten dinner, she decided that she would sit and watch a movie with them. She had been so preoccupied with her issues, that she hadn't really spent any quality time with them. She would normally just stick them in the room with Raven or Penny Proud and call it day.

Cherise allowed Alysa and Alyson to pick the movie they were going to watch, out of their collection of DVDs, and as always, Alysa would be the one to pick the movie. Alyson didn't care what they watched, she was just happy to have girl time.

They snuggled up on the couch and began to watch *The Parent Trap*. Lindsay Lohan did an outstanding job playing the dual role of identical twins separated by their parent's divorce, while they were still babies. Nick and Elizabeth decided to split the kids fifty-fifty. He would take one and raise her in Napa Valley and Elizabeth would take the other and raise her in London. It just so happened that they ended up at the same summer camp, and after removing their masks after a fencing match, they were surprised to see their face on the other.

Before the end of camp, the plot to break up their father's engagement to the beautiful "Cruella", and restore their parents and family as one began. Loads of laughter filled the living room. Before they could finish the movie, Terrell came by to share his good news.

Terrell's tour was almost over, and he had been applying for jobs. He was so excited when he received a call for an interview for a company in Savannah, Georgia. He came home to get some documents and clothes needed for the interview. He debated whether he should tell Cherise, but decided to stop by and tell her anyway. When she heard the news, she wanted to scream, but she played it off like she was happy for him.

They hadn't really talked much since she'd been served with the divorce papers, but whenever he was home, he would pick the girls up and let them spend the night with him. Cherise never fought against it, because whether she and Terrell worked out their problems, she still wanted him to be a part of the girls' life.

After Terrell left, she waited for the movie to end, and once she got the girls situated for bed, she called Lauren for consolation. Her heart was heavy from having to go through the divorce class. She was still praying, fasting and confessing, but having to go through the class was just one more valid proof that the divorce was almost about to happen.

On top of that, she just received the news about Terrell possibly getting a job and moving closer to Toni. She wanted to give up, but Lauren encouraged her to hold on. After they had prayed, Cherise retired to her room and fell on her knees and continued to talk to the Lord.

Lord, I just don't understand. I'm doing all that I know to do. I've been fasting. I've been confessing. I've been trusting, and I don't know what else to do. You said that if I ask anything, believing and not doubting, it shall be so, and I've been doing just that.

How can my marriage be restored if Terrell moves to Savannah? Separation is not good for a marriage, Lord. Even You said it in your Word. Lord, I'm asking that even though he has the interview; don't allow him to get the job. Please protect my marriage, and give me strength to endure. I thank You for all that You've done, and all that You are going to do. Thank you for restoring my marriage, in Jesus name, Amen

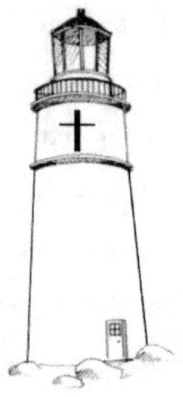

Chapter Thirty-One

Cherise sat in the car on her lunch break and pulled out her Bible. As she turned the pages, she began to pray, "Lord, thank you for restoring my marriage. Today is not a good day. I am sooo weak. Your Word says that your strength is made perfect in my weakness. I guess that means you are doing your best work on my behalf today. I need your strength to carry me through this day."

She looked down and noticed a scripture that read, "Therefore do not worry about tomorrow, for tomorrow will worry about itself."

Before she could finish reading the entire scripture, she retorted, "Lord, I'm not worrying about tomorrow, I need help getting through today."

She continued reading, "Each day has enough trouble of its own."

"You can say that again. Today is like WHEW!"

She tried to hold back the tears, but the words to the song now playing on her homemade CD was ministering to her weakened soul. She had taken different songs from original artists' albums that ministered faith and compiled them on one disc and entitled it, Keeper of My Soul.

These songs kept her through the midst of what she was going through. Songs like "Thou Art a Shield for Me" by Byron Cage gave encouragement and peace during the storm. Songs like "I Will Bless Your Name" by Paull Graham encouraged her to worship God in spite of what she was feeling and in spite of what she was going through. "I Need You Now" by Smokie Norful expressed the urgency she felt during this trial. She was literally on the edge and was about to break in any minute. Her crisis was an emergency and she needed God to respond immediately. Prophetic songs by Kimberly and Alberto Rivera spoke life to her dead situations and always gave a sense of refreshing after leading her into another realm of worship. They were the type of songs that she needed during this time in her life. She found comfort in their words, and no matter where she went or what she was doing—this was her CD of choice.

Right now she was listening to Donnie Mcclurkin's "I'll Trust You Lord." Every time she heard it, she couldn't help but wonder what the inspiration behind it was. Donnie must have experienced something that required him to totally trust God, despite what the situation looked like. Whatever it was, she was grateful because, it always gave her the strength she needed to hold on just a little while longer.

When lunch was over, she retreated back to her desk to bury herself in work, in hopes that it would help pass the time away. She hadn't been seated any more than fifteen minutes when she received the phone call from Terrell, advising her that he got the job. She faked her excitement as best she could and congratulated him on his good news. She rushed him off the phone by pretending that she had to go into a meeting.

She didn't quite lie because she did go into a meeting, but not the type of meeting that she would normally be referring to. She walked into one of the conference rooms and locked the door. She fell on her knees and began to cry out to the Lord. She told Him how hurt she was, but no matter what, she would trust Him. When she didn't know what else to say, she began to pray in the spirit and offer up praises unto the Lord. From the pits of her belly, she felt a surge of strength that she never knew resided within her. She stood up from her knees and in mid praise, turned her attention to the devil.

"I DON'T CARE WHAT YOU DO. I WILL NOT BOW DOWN TO YOU. I SERVE GOD AND ONLY HE WILL I SERVE. SO EVEN IF HE MOVES AWAY, I WILL STILL TRUST AND SERVE GOD. EVEN IF MY MARRIAGE IS NOT RESTORED, I WILL STILL TRUST AND SERVE GOD. EVEN IF HE GETS REMARRIED, I WILL STILL TRUST AND SERVE GOD. DO YOU HEAR ME? I... WILL... NOT... BOW... DOWN... TO... YOU.

In a matter of seconds, Cherise's mourning had turned into praises. She no longer felt the heaviness of her burdens, but was surrounded by a real peace that surpassed her understanding. She opened the door to the conference room and walked out with a smile. She couldn't explain what had just transpired in the meeting, but she knew that she had been delivered from all that vexed her.

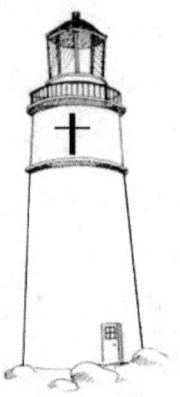

Chapter Thirty-Two

Lauren was so excited about Cherise's testimony regarding what had transpired in her meeting today. They'd talked the entire time Cherise was driving home from work. Even after Cherise stopped to pick up the kids, Lauren patiently held on the line. When Cherise pulled into the driveway of their home, she allowed Alyson to open the door, so she and Alysa could go ahead in the house while she went to the mailbox to get the mail.

Still talking to Lauren, she flipped through the mail and stopped when she saw an envelope addressed to her from the Clerk of Court. Just as she figured, it was her divorce hearing date. She allowed Lauren to finish what she was talking about before telling her.

"Guess what I just got," Cherise said to Lauren with a hint of excitement in her voice.

"A check?"

"No, guess again."

"I don't know, tell me."

"I just got my divorce hearing in the mail."

"Aw, I'm sorry, Cherise."

"I'm not. I'm not even worried about this piece of paper." Cherise couldn't explain it, but ever since the meeting she had today in the conference room, her faith level was registering full.

"Oh wow," Lauren said with amazement. She was impressed at Cherise's confidence. "I'm surprised at how well you're taking this."

"I can't explain it, but I'm truly not worried about it. I'm trusting God."

"All I can say is wow. When is the hearing?"

"May 25th."

"That's only three weeks away."

"Yeah I know."

"Are you going to go?"

"You know what? I kinda feel like Abraham right now."

"How's that?"

"God told Abraham to go and sacrifice his son. I'm sure Abraham was devastated by God's request. I can imagine how he must have felt. Here God is telling him to go and kill the son that He promised him. And not only that…"

"Yeah?" Lauren queried, desiring to hear more of Cherise's story.

"See, God told Abraham, if you go and read a few chapters back, I think somewhere in chapter seventeen, that He was going to establish His covenant with his son by Sarah and his son's seed. As a matter of fact, He called Isaac by name." Cherise paced back and forth in the yard as she continued telling the story.

"Anyhoo, Abraham moved in obedience to God's request, but I believe he was holding God to what he had previously promised him. Why? Because God is not a man that He should lie, nor the son of man that He should repent, right?"

"Right," Lauren agreed.

"Right. God can't lie. So check this out. As Abraham, Isaac and his men approached the place where he would sacrifice his son, Abraham told his men to stay back with the asses, and he and the lad was going to worship and they would return. Right there, he was speaking faith. How would he and the lad return if he was supposed to sacrifice the boy?"

"Yeah, that's sure nuff faith," Lauren added.

"Right, but check this out." Cherise was on a roll. Her excitement excited Lauren. "On their way to their destination, Isaac asked Abraham, "Hey dad, you got the fire and you got the wood, but where's the sacrifice?" Cherise paraphrased Isaac's statement to sound more Twenty-first Centuryish. "And Abraham told him that God would provide for himself a lamb. That was faith. I'm pretty sure Abraham was saying, 'Even if I sacrifice my boy, God will have to perform some type of miracle to give him back to me because He promised.' Lauren, God promised me something, and even if the divorce goes through, I believe God will perform a miracle in the end."

"Woo Hoo," Lauren screamed through the phone. "Cherise that was awesome. You are going to be an excellent teacher slash preacher someday. I mean, that was truly amazing."

"Aw girl, stop."

"I'm for real, Cherise. You should have heard yourself."

Cherise laughed as Lauren imitated her. They enjoyed a few more laughs and Cherise walked in the house to spend an enjoyable evening with her girls.

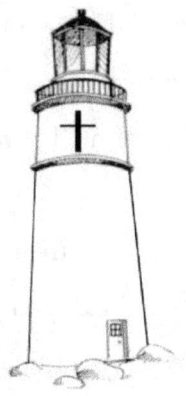

Chapter Thirty-Three

"Happy Mother's Day, Mom," Alyson and Alysa announced as they walked in their mother's room carrying their version of breakfast in bed. Alyson carried a plate with two toaster strudels on it, and Alysa carried a cup which contained orange juice. Alyson wasn't able to use the stove without supervision, but she had one hundred percent clearance on the toaster. It was either toast or toaster strudels, and plain toast didn't seem too appetizing to Alyson.

Cherise was elated by her babies' creativity. She sat the plate and cup on her night stand and held out her arms to offer hugs and kisses. The two girls jumped in their mother's bed, one on each side, and hugged her at the same time.

After a delicious breakfast, Cherise and the girls dressed for church. Cherise didn't normally buy a new outfit for Mother's Day, but with all the weight she had lost from fasting, she had to. She looked good, if she had to say so herself.

Mother's Day was always special at the Harvest and there was no telling what type of surprise they could expect today. As they were getting in the car, Terrell pulled in behind them with balloons and a gift in hand.

"Happy Mother's Day," Terrell said as he handed Cherise the balloons and gift.

"Wow, I don't know what to say. I really didn't expect this."

"Um, thank you would be nice."

"Oh, forgive me. Thank you."

"Well, are you going to open your gift or what?"

"Oh, okay." Cherise passed the balloons to the girls and unwrapped the nicely gift wrapped box. *What on earth could this be?* Cherise's mouth dropped as she opened the box. When she looked up, Terrell was down on one knee.

"I didn't take the job. It took me every bit of ten minutes to call them back and thank them for offering it to me, but, then I told them I had to decline the offer. As soon as I hung up the phone with you, I knew this is where I was supposed to be. I'm sorry for all that I've put you through, and if you will have me, I would like to come back home."

"Ah…ah…" Cherise was speechless.

"I kept your ring, but I can get you a new one if you want."

Cherise was surprised that Terrell still had her ring. She had packed it with the rest of his clothes, when she first had him put out. She had sworn that she would never wear that ring again because it had no more meaning. She had even declared that if they ever got back together, he would have to get her a new one.

Once again she had to eat her words. When she opened the box, the old ring looked like new. *Old things are passed away; behold all things are become new.* It had been cleaned and it sparkled even brighter than it did on their wedding day.

"Ah…ah…"

"I've arranged with Pastor Revenew to renew our vows today during the services. Will you remarry me?

"Ah…ah…"

"YES," Alyson yelled.

"Yes," Alysa repeated, copying her big sister's excitement.

"That's two, but I need one more," Terrell insisted.

"Oh my God! Is this for real? Are you serious?"

"As a heart attack. So can you please answer so I can stand up because I'm getting my pants dirty down here?"

"Um, I guess. I mean...What about To—?"

Before she could finish pronouncing Toni's name, Terrell interrupted her. "You don't have to worry about that. It's already taken care of," he assured.

"What about the divorce hearing? It's only two weeks away."

"If you say yes, I plan on calling them tomorrow and cancel the divorce. So whatta you say? Will you remarry me?"

Cherise looked Terrell in his eyes to see if she could detect a hint of dishonesty, but she didn't. She then looked at Alyson, then finally Alysa, and she could tell by their smiles that they approved. Without any further reservations she answered, "Yes."

Terrell stood and pulled Cherise in his embrace. Tears of joy ran down both of their faces. As the girls clapped and screamed, Terrell passionately kissed his wife as if this was his first time.

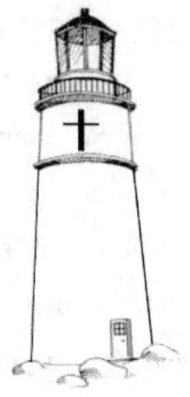

Chapter Thirty-Four

This was the best Mother's Day ever. Her babies served her breakfast in bed, Terrell was coming back home, and most importantly, God had answered her prayers. God had shown Himself faithful.

As Cherise exhorted the people and told her short testimony, a soft melody was birthed in her spirit. She began to sing a worship from her heart.

You are so faithful, I love You Jesus.
You are so faithful, I adore You.
You are so faithful, I give You praise.
You are so faithful, I exalt Your name.

You are so fa-aith-ful. Looooord, You are so faaaith-ful.
You are so fa-aith-ful. Ooooooh, You are so faaaith-ful.

Cherise lifted her right hand and allowed it to fall and rest on her chest to express her passion and love for God. When her hand felt the cross that she wore around her neck, she remembered her grandmother and released a smile. Without missing a beat, she transitioned right into the song Ms. Mamie sang to her the day she'd given her the necklace. She now knew why her grandmother was crying that day. She must have had her own experience with God, and found him to be faithful as well. Cherise now knew the true meaning to the old spiritual hymn.

Cherise could tell Terrell had put a lot of careful thought and energy into planning this day. The renewal of the vows was a dream come true, and to Cherise's surprise, everyone was there—including Sasha, Sybill and their husbands. Cherise couldn't be sure, but she could have sworn she saw Sybill shed a few tears.

By the end of service, Sybill and her husband had given their lives to the Lord. They had experienced a great move of God in the life of their friend, and if they were going to serve any god, Cherise's God would be the one. Where there was doubt, they now believed. Cherise couldn't ask for much more.

After church, everyone went out to dinner, and the night ended with Terrell moving some of his clothes back into the house. After everyone had fallen asleep, Cherise remembered that she hadn't spoken with Lauren today and decided to call her. Although it was late in Georgia, it was still pretty early in California with the three hour time difference.

"I knew it. I just knew it!" Lauren screamed with excitement by the news Cherise shared with her. "I knew God was going to do it for you, Cherise." She was so happy for her friend. She praised God with as much enthusiasm she could conjure up.

Even though she had not heard from Jeff in a while, she dared not be jealous of what the Lord had done for Cherise. It hadn't happened for her yet, but she was still standing and believing God for restoration. Cherise had given her hope, and she knew that God was not a respectetr of persons. If he did it for Cherise, He could definitely do it for her too.

Ater hanging up from Lauren, Cherise retreated to her favorite room in the house and drew a bath. As she reclined back and allowed her body to be overtaken by the relaxing waters, she found herself back on another rollercoaster ride as she thought about all she had gone through. She recalled all the hurt, the anguish, the tears, and the anger. In the end, although it was painful, it was worth it.

She thought about Abraham and imagined the joy he must have felt when he saw the ram in the bush. His faith carried him all the way to the end of his journey and God showed up just in the nick of time. God was truly faithful.

She thought about Toni and felt a sense of sadness. Just as she predicted, Toni had indeed taken Terrell back after he lied, and even after she knew he was married. More than likely, he sold her a dream worth believing in.

As a woman, Cherise knew how it felt to be heartbroken, and she didn't wish that type of pain on anyone. She offered up a prayer for the woman who almost had taken her husband from her. She asked God to forgive her, heal her and bless her with a loving husband of her own.

For a moment she laughed at some of the craziest things she did during her trial. Even some of the prayers she prayed were just as outrageous such as, asking the Lord to not allow Terrell to get an erection when he was around Toni. She was sure God got a kick out of some of things he heard. As silly as it sounded now, she was one-hundred percent serious when she prayed it. Hey, what was a desperate girl supposed to do?

She was amazed at the love of God permeating through her heart. It overruled all the hate she had built up towards Terrell and it overlooked the fact that Toni was sleeping with her husband. The more she prayed, fasted and stayed in the Word, the more she saw change in her life. God had done open heart surgery on her, right before her eyes. He had taken away her heart of stone and given her a heart of flesh.

In order for her to do ministry, God needed her to see people the way He saw them—not through her eyes, but His. He needed her to love people the way He loved them—not with her heart, but His. When it was hard and even when it hurt, He caused her to love like He would.

The more she thought about God's love she realized; God's love has no boundaries and God's love has no end. His love never gives up on a person or a situation, and no matter what, His love somehow—always endures forever.

Cherise could clearly see that had it not been for this trial, she would have not sought the Lord as fervently as she did. Now looking back on things, she realized that God used her mess to birth ministry in her. The battle wasn't about Terrell or their marriage at all, it was really all about her—getting her to the place God was calling her to—the purpose for which He had created her.

All things work together for good to them that love God, to them who are called according to His purpose. God had taken her mess and created a beautiful message of hope for her to share with others. Remembering the dream that started her journey, she was now prepared and ready to be a lifesaver to the world.

Book Club/Reading Group Questions

1. What did you think this book was about before you read it? Were your thoughts, right?

2. What do you think about it now that you've actually read it?

3. Did you see yourself in this book? If so, how?

4. What situations in the book helped you?

5. In the beginning of the book, Cherise had a dream about her husband. Does God ever speak to you in your dreams? What was the dream? Do you know the meaning? Have you sought the Lord for the meaning?

6. Write down a time when you needed God to move in a situation.

7. Have you ever wanted something and prayed for it only to discover you were the one God wanted to change?

8. What are you willing to sacrifice to get what you want?

9. How did the friends help or hinder Cherise in her journey to reconciliation? How do your friends help or hinder you in growing closer to God?

10. Have you ever found yourself tempted by the counterfeit while you were praying for the "real thing"?

11. Have you ever blamed God for circumstances in your life? If so, what? How do you feel about it now?

12. Do you think Cherise should have divorced Terrell? Why or why not?

13. Would you have gone through the fire as Cherise did? At what point would you have given up?

14. Do you trust God?

15. Have you ever given up on a situation or God? Do you regret it?

16. Have you ever had to rely solely on God for anything? If so, what? What was the outcome?

17. What did you think of Cherise's "realness"? Do you find it hard to be real and a Christian?

18. What's the worst thing(s) anyone has ever done to you? Have you forgiven them?

19. Would you recommend this book to anyone? If so, who and why?

20. If you could say or ask anything to the author of this book, what would it be? (Now take this time to send her the message via her contacts and don't forget to go to Amazon, Barnes & Nobles, Goodreads.com, etc and leave a review.

www.ingramcontent.com/pod-product-compliance
Lightning Source LLC
Chambersburg PA
CBHW070107260626
47160CB00004B/1356